BINKY

TAKES CHARGE

KIDS CAN PRESS

For Meggy, Ethan, their kitties and the puppy I hope they get some day

Text and illustrations © 2012 Ashley Spires

Kids Can Press acknowledges the financial support of the Government of Ontario, through the
Ontario Media Development Corporation's Ontario Book Initiative; the Ontario Arts Council;
the Canada Council for the Arts; and the Government of Canada, through the BPIDP, for our
publishing activity.

Published in Canada by
Kids Can Press Ltd.
25 Dockside Drive
Toronto, ON M5A 0B5

Published in the U.S. by
Kids Can Press Ltd.
2250 Military Road
Tonawanda, NY 14150

www.kidscanpress.com

The artwork in this book was rendered in ink, watercolor, cat fur, bits of kitty litter,
the occasional paw print and dog slobber.
The text is set in Fontoon.

Edited by Tara Walker and Karen Li
Series designer: Karen Powers
Designed by Rachel Di Salle

The hardcover edition of this book is smyth sewn casebound.
The paperback edition of this book is limp sewn with a drawn-on cover.
Manufactured in Shen Zhen, Guang Dong, P.R. China, in 4/2012 by Printplus Limited.

CM 12 0 9 8 7 6 5 4 3 2 1
CM PA 12 0 9 8 7 6 5 4 3 2 1

Library and Archives Canada Cataloguing in Publication

Spires, Ashley, 1978–
        Binky takes charge / by Ashley Spires.   Juvenile
                                                    GRAPHIC
(A Binky adventure)   Binky 2
ISBN 978-1-55453-703-7 (bound)   ISBN 978-1-55453-768-6 (pbk.)

        I. Title. II. Series: Spire, Ashley, 1978– . Binky adventure.

PS8637.P57B552 2012   jC813'.6   C2012-900815-X

Kids Can Press is a ℓℓℓ(©ℓℓ)ℓℓ𝗦™ Entertainment company

NO CARPETS WERE PEED ON IN THE MAKING OF THIS BOOK. THERE WAS A HAIRBALL ON THE STAIRS, A SERIOUS CASE OF KITTY-LITTER FOOT AND ONE MYSTERIOUS POO NUGGET IN THE BEDROOM, BUT ALL RUGS REMAINED DRY AND URINE-FREE.

BINKY

TAKES CHARGE

by ASHLEY SPIRES

tick tock

IT ALL STARTS TODAY.

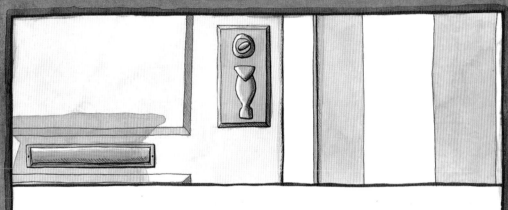

A WHOLE NEW MISSION.

A WHOLE NEW ADVENTURE.

A WHOLE NEW SPACE CAT.

OR AT LEAST THERE WILL BE WHEN BINKY IS DONE TRAINING HIM.

BINKY IS NO ORDINARY HOUSE CAT ...

prrrrrr

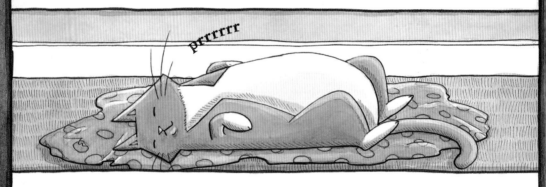

OR EVEN AN EVERYDAY SPACE CAT.

MEORRR!

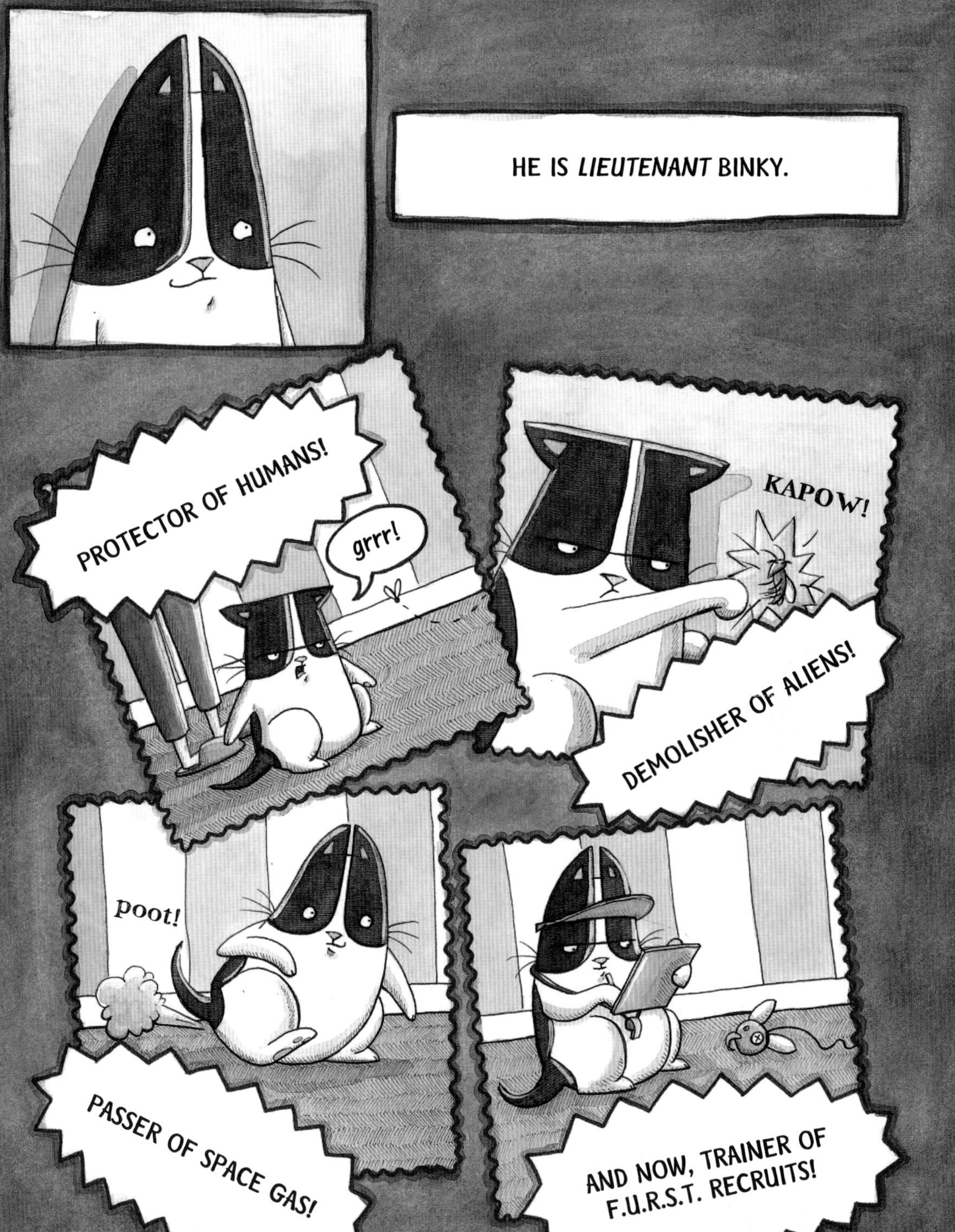

HE IS *LIEUTENANT* BINKY.
PROTECTOR OF HUMANS!
grrr!
KAPOW!
DEMOLISHER OF ALIENS!
poot!
PASSER OF SPACE GAS!
AND NOW, TRAINER OF F.U.R.S.T. RECRUITS!

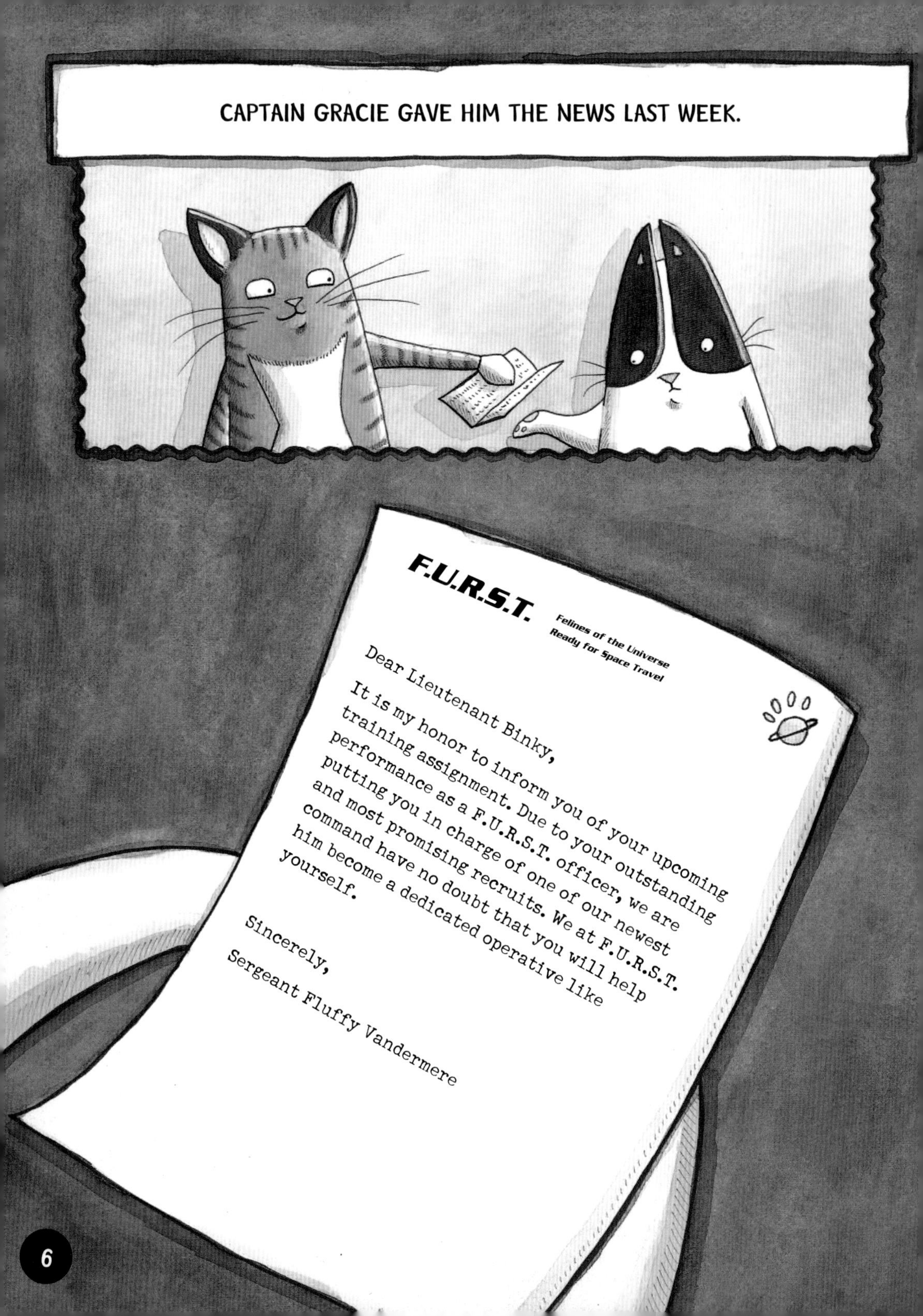
CAPTAIN GRACIE GAVE HIM THE NEWS LAST WEEK.
F.U.R.S.T.
Felines of the Universe
Ready for Space Travel
Dear Lieutenant Binky,
It is my honor to inform you of your upcoming training assignment. Due to your outstanding performance as a F.U.R.S.T. officer, we are putting you in charge of one of our newest and most promising recruits. We at F.U.R.S.T. command have no doubt that you will help him become a dedicated operative like yourself.
Sincerely,
Sergeant Fluffy Vandermere

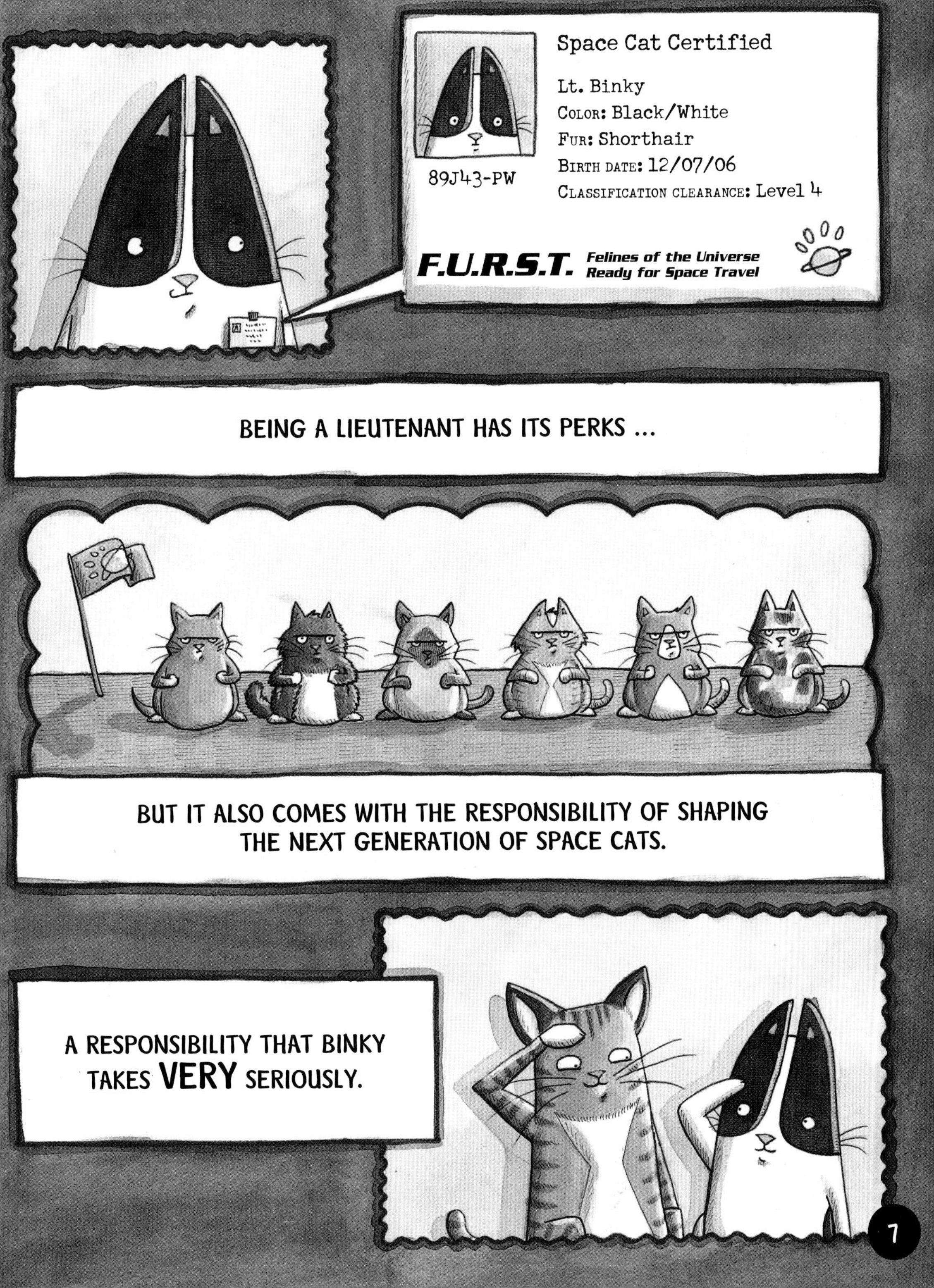
Space Cat Certified
Lt. Binky
COLOR: Black/White
FUR: Shorthair
BIRTH DATE: 12/07/06
CLASSIFICATION CLEARANCE: Level 4
89J43-PW
F.U.R.S.T. Felines of the Universe Ready for Space Travel
BEING A LIEUTENANT HAS ITS PERKS ...
BUT IT ALSO COMES WITH THE RESPONSIBILITY OF SHAPING THE NEXT GENERATION OF SPACE CATS.
A RESPONSIBILITY THAT BINKY TAKES VERY SERIOUSLY.

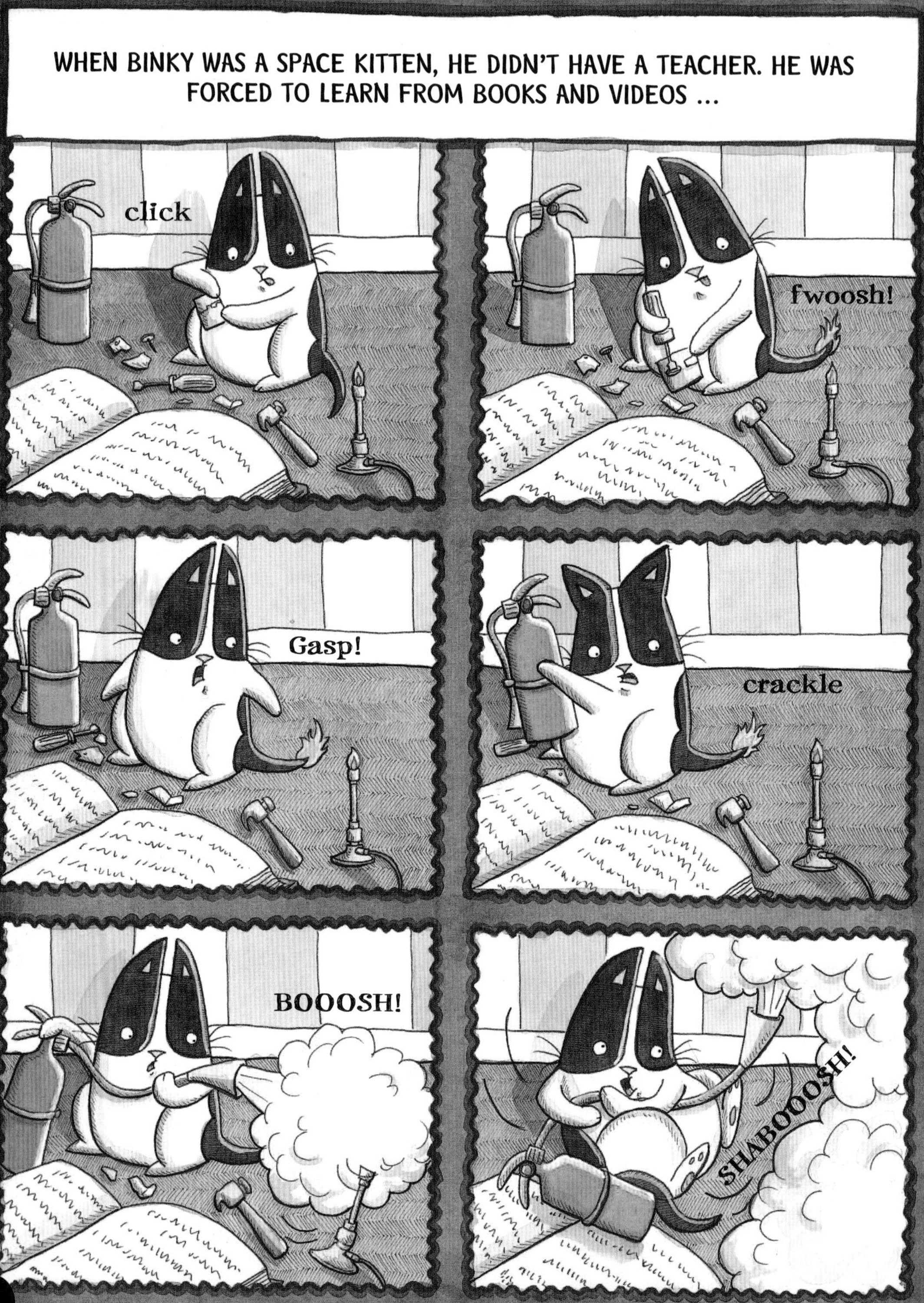
WHEN BINKY WAS A SPACE KITTEN, HE DIDN'T HAVE A TEACHER. HE WAS FORCED TO LEARN FROM BOOKS AND VIDEOS ...
click
fwoosh!
Gasp!
crackle
BOOOSH!
SHABOOOSH!

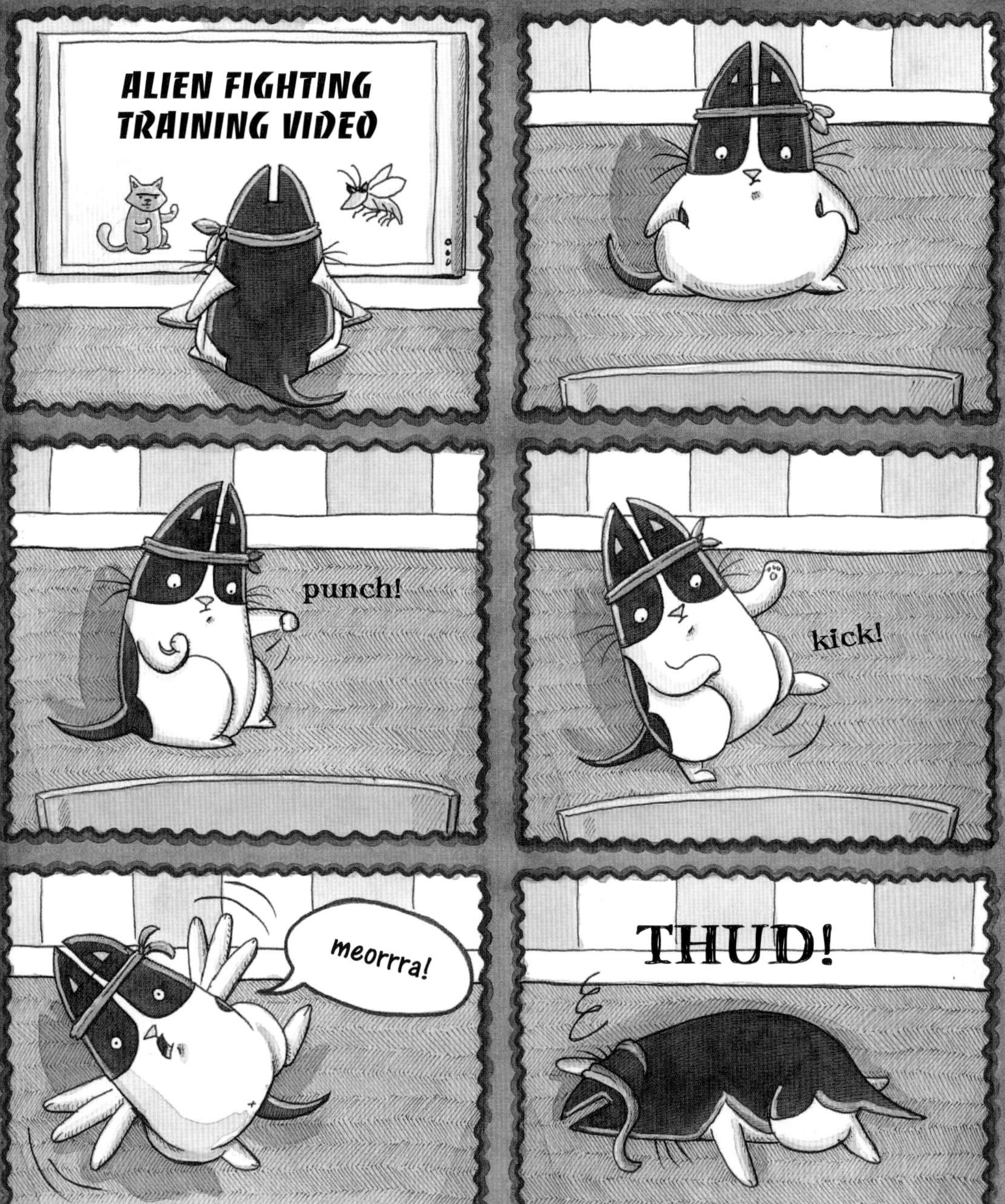
ALIEN FIGHTING
TRAINING VIDEO
punch!
kick!
meorrra!
THUD!
WHICH TURNED OUT TO BE A BIT CHALLENGING.

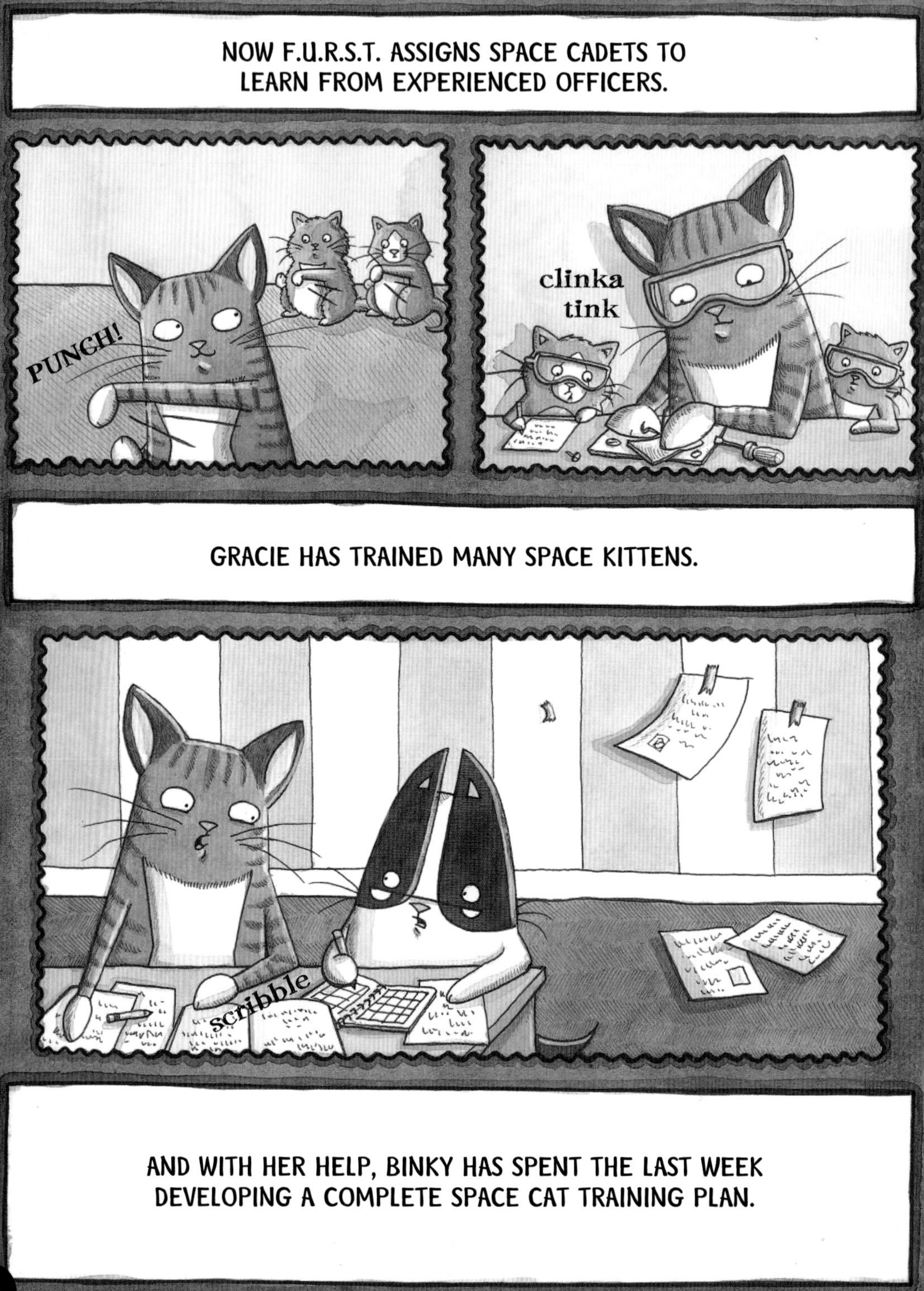
NOW F.U.R.S.T. ASSIGNS SPACE CADETS TO LEARN FROM EXPERIENCED OFFICERS.
PUNCH!
clinka tink
GRACIE HAS TRAINED MANY SPACE KITTENS.
scribble
AND WITH HER HELP, BINKY HAS SPENT THE LAST WEEK DEVELOPING A COMPLETE SPACE CAT TRAINING PLAN.

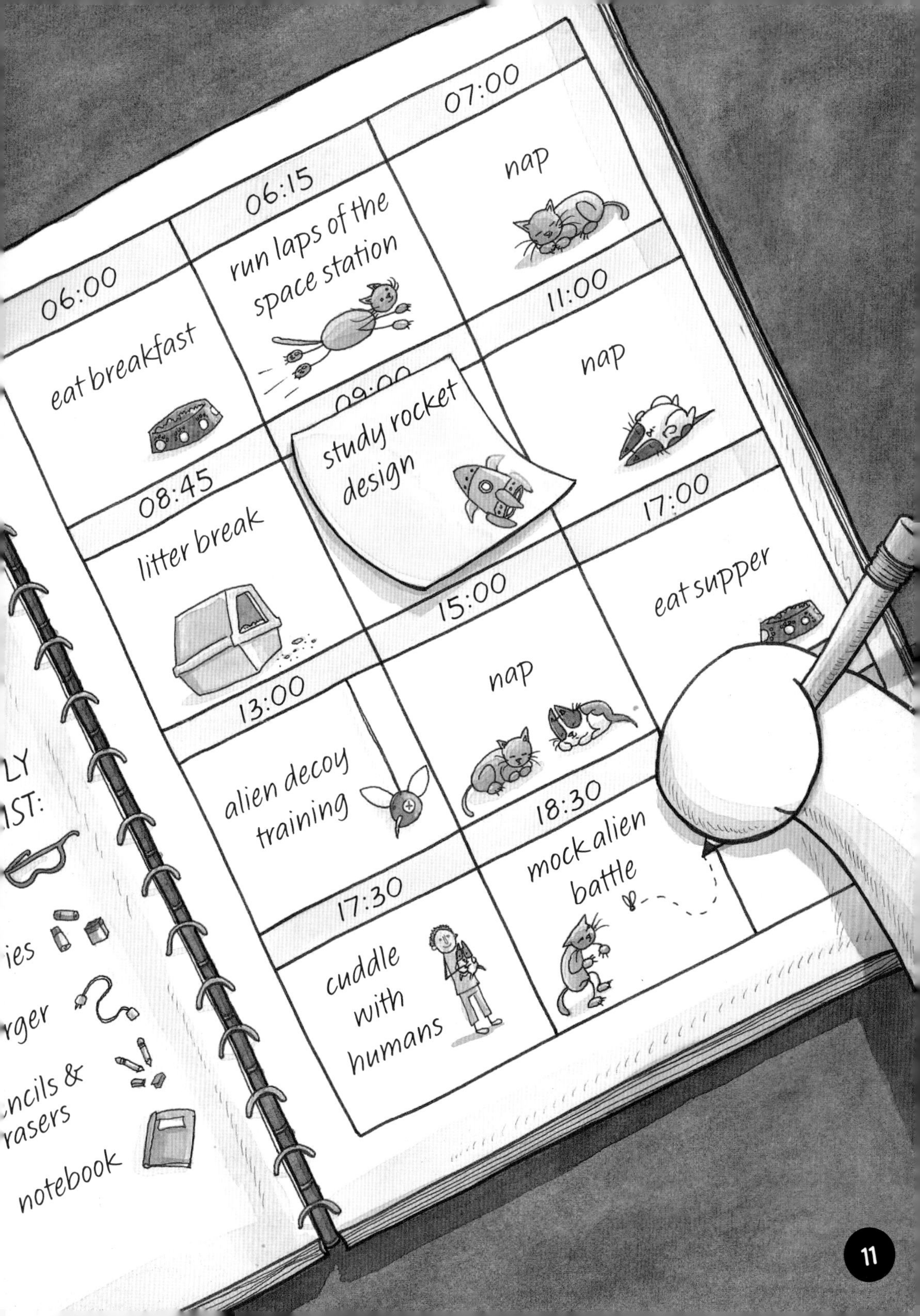
06:00
eat breakfast
06:15
run laps of the space station
07:00
nap
11:00
nap
09:00
study rocket design
08:45
litter break
17:00
eat supper
15:00
nap
13:00
alien decoy training
18:30
mock alien battle
17:30
cuddle with humans
LY
IST:
ies
rger
ncils &
rasers
notebook

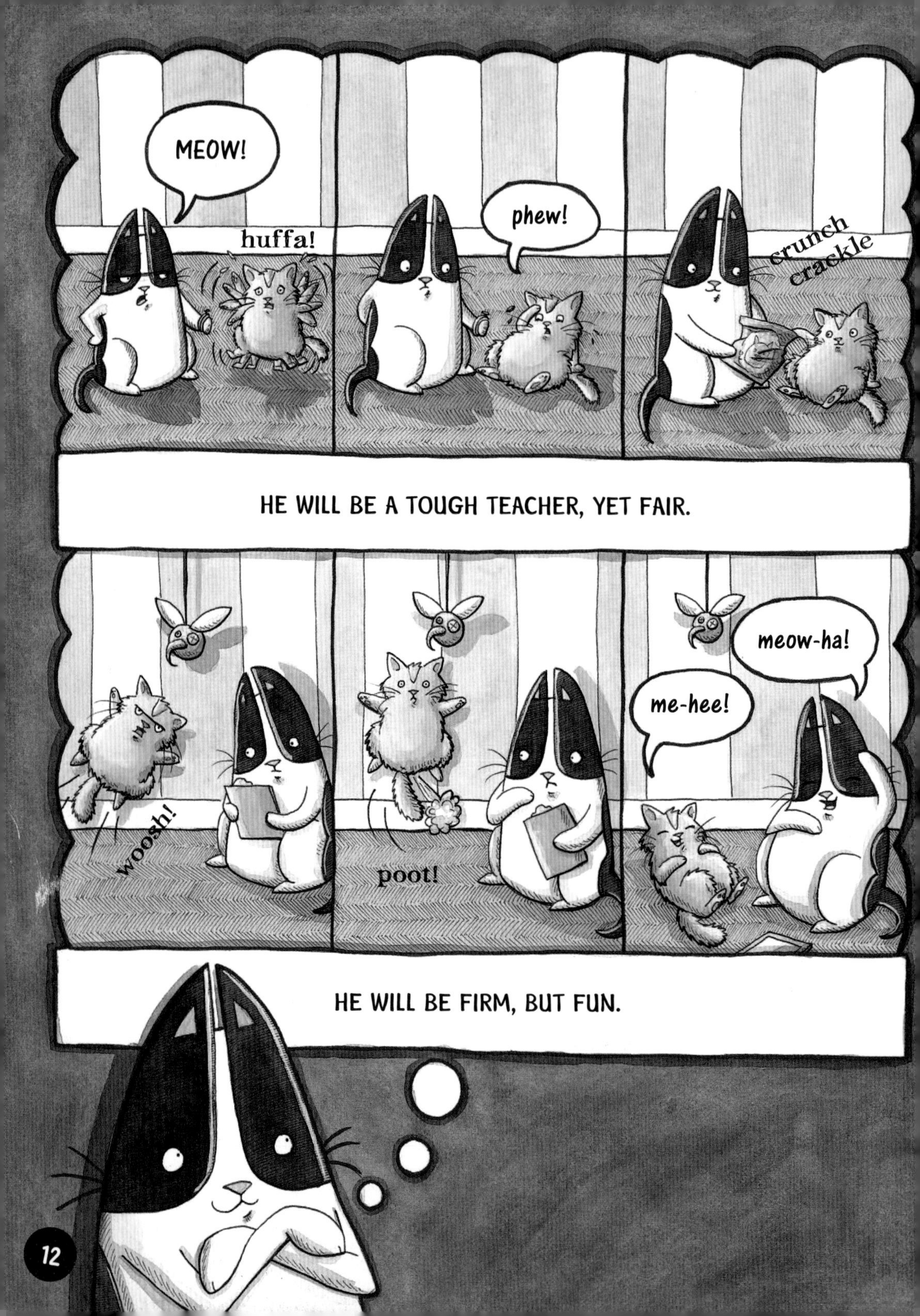

MEOW!
huffa!
phew!
crunch
crackle
HE WILL BE A TOUGH TEACHER, YET FAIR.
woosh!
poot!
me-hee!
meow-ha!
HE WILL BE FIRM, BUT FUN.

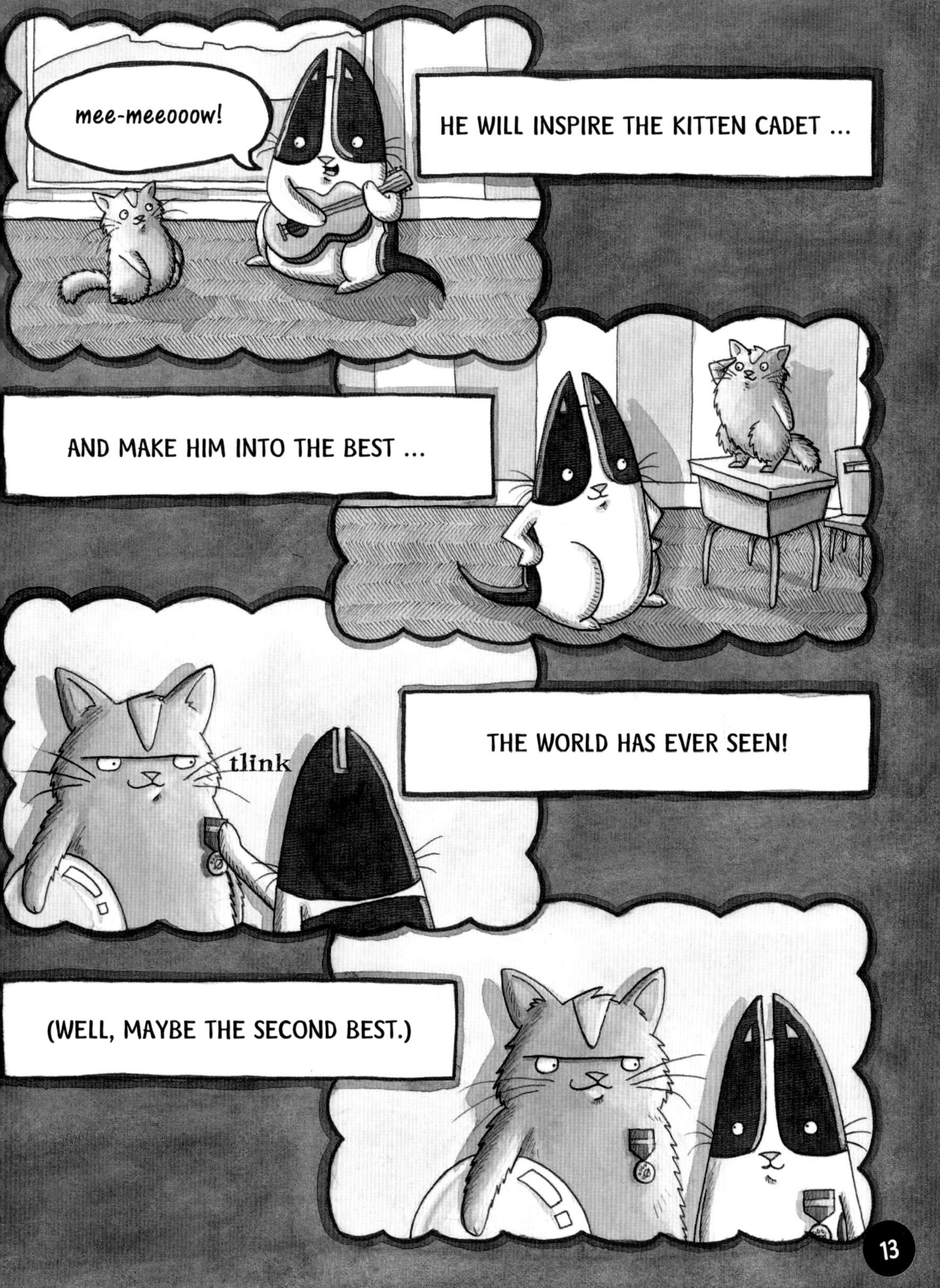
mee-meeooow!
HE WILL INSPIRE THE KITTEN CADET ...
AND MAKE HIM INTO THE BEST ...
tlink
THE WORLD HAS EVER SEEN!
(WELL, MAYBE THE SECOND BEST.)

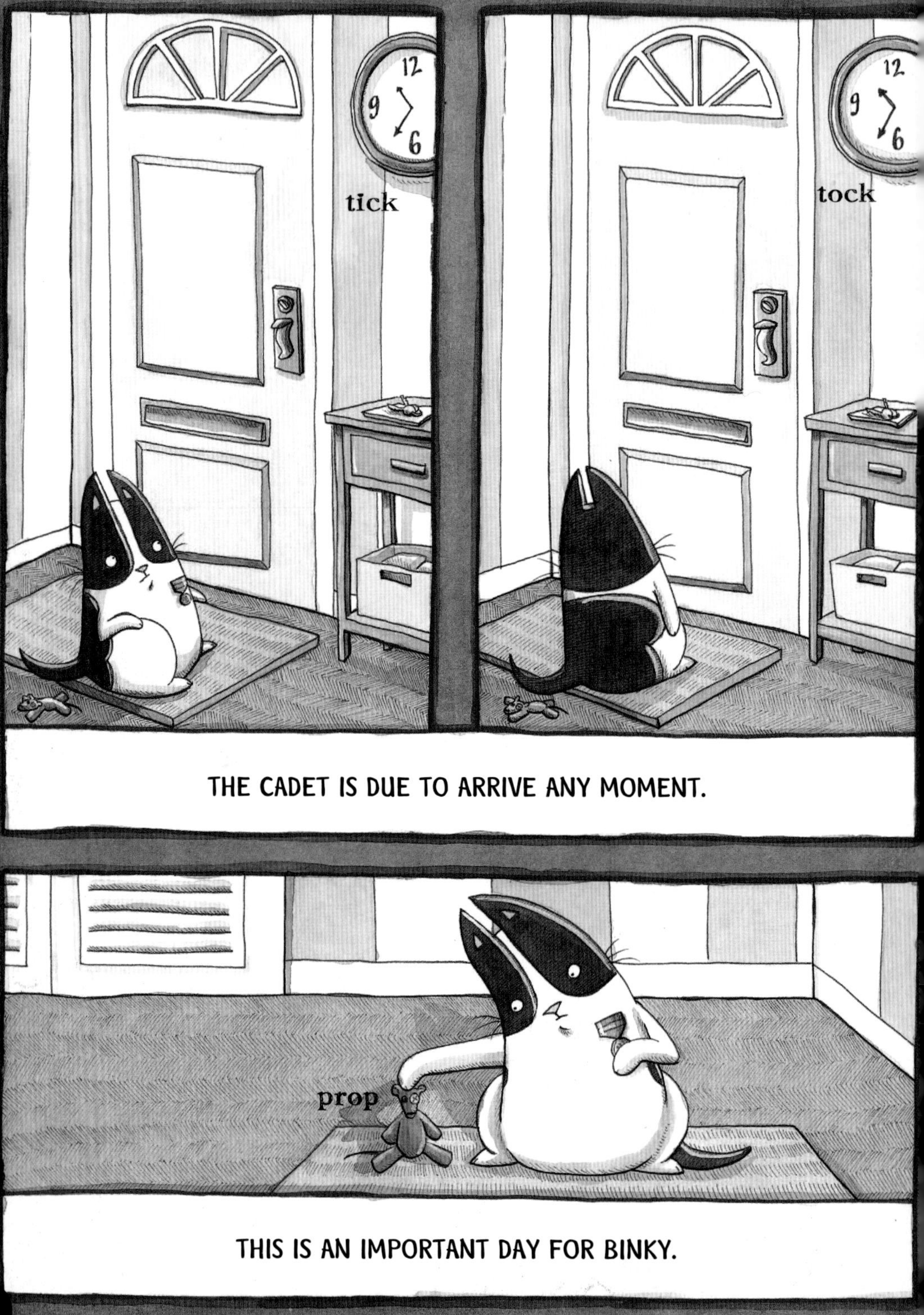
tick
tock
THE CADET IS DUE TO ARRIVE ANY MOMENT.
prop
THIS IS AN IMPORTANT DAY FOR BINKY.

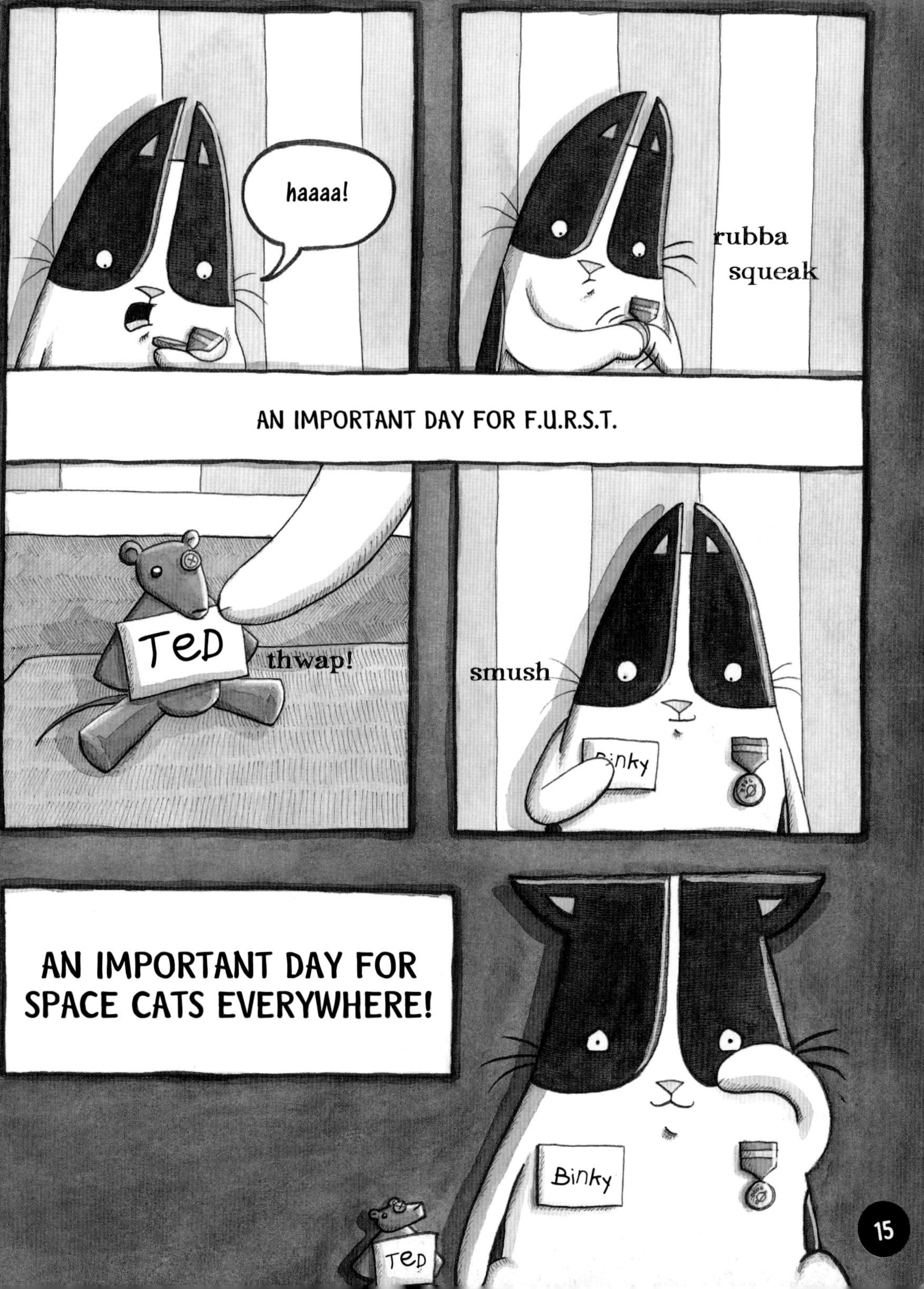

haaaa!
rubba
squeak
AN IMPORTANT DAY FOR F.U.R.S.T.
TED
thwap!
smush
Binky
AN IMPORTANT DAY FOR
SPACE CATS EVERYWHERE!
Binky
TED

DING! DONG!

HE'S HERE!

Oh, he's so cute!

Look how fuzzy he is!

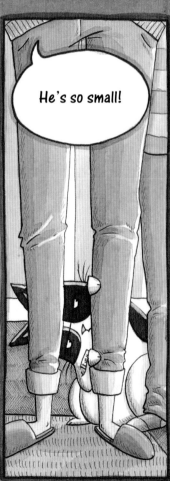

He's so small!

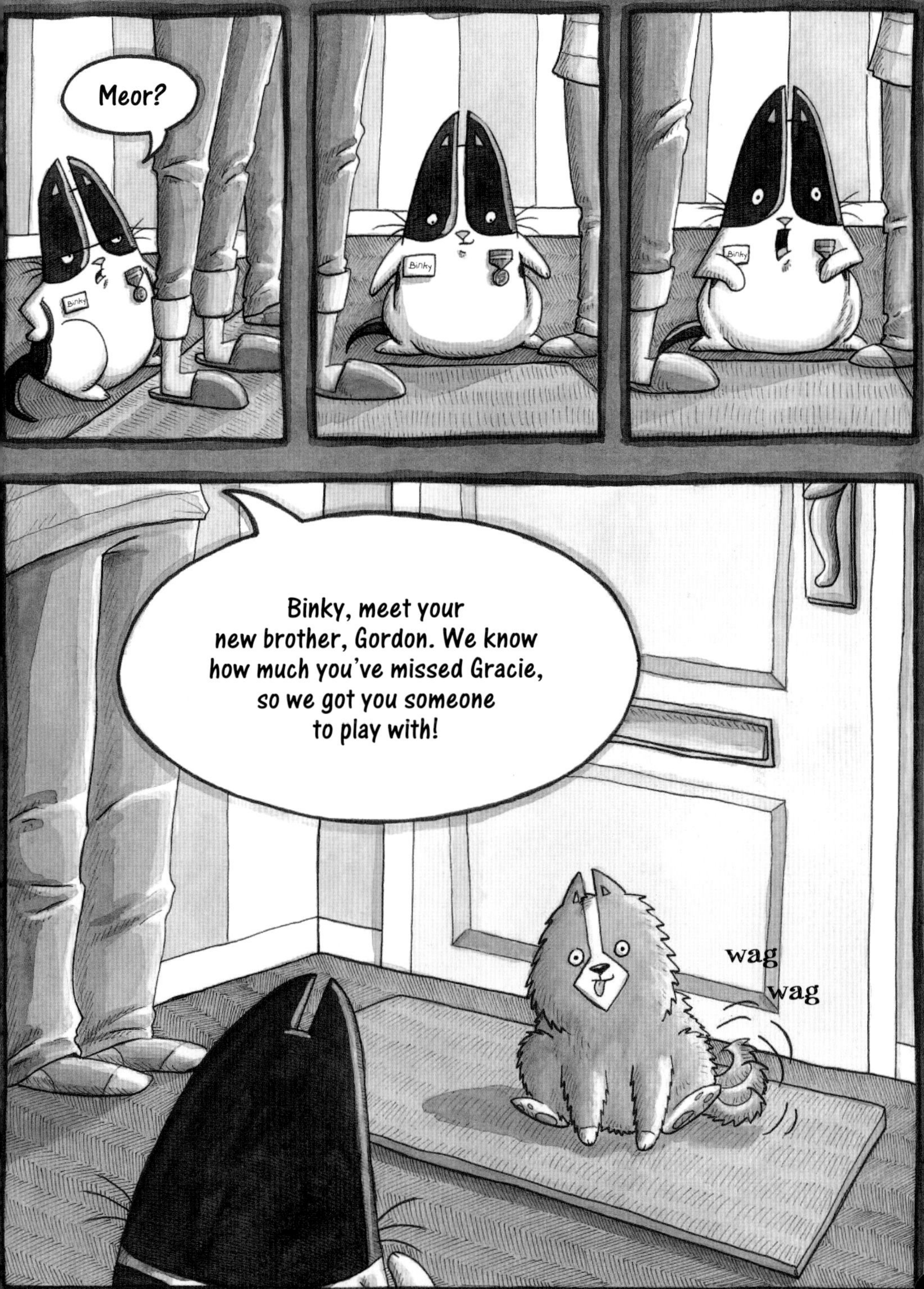
Meor?
Binky
Binky
Binky
Binky, meet your new brother, Gordon. We know how much you've missed Gracie, so we got you someone to play with!
wag
wag

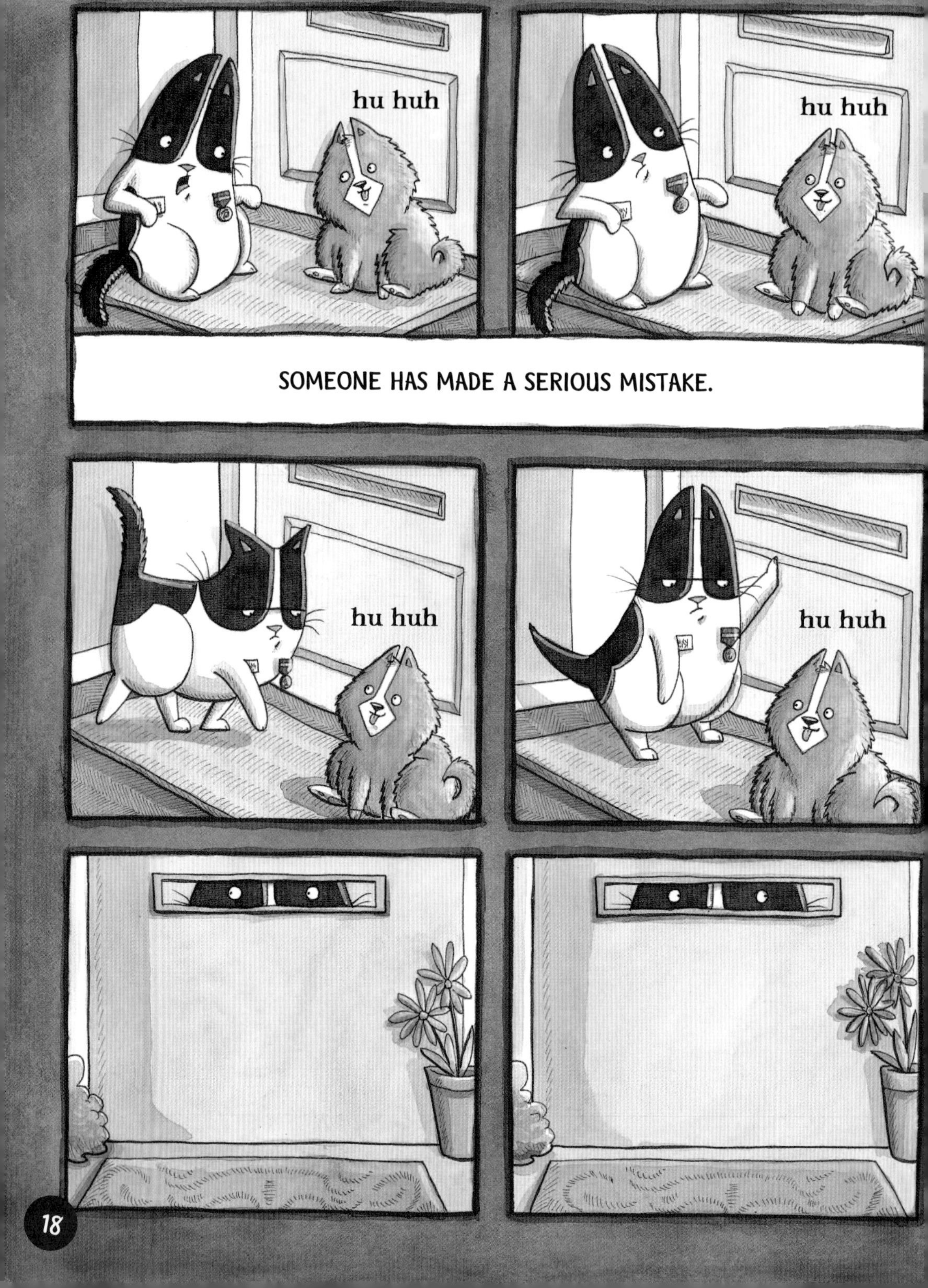
hu huh
hu huh
SOMEONE HAS MADE A SERIOUS MISTAKE.
hu huh
hu huh

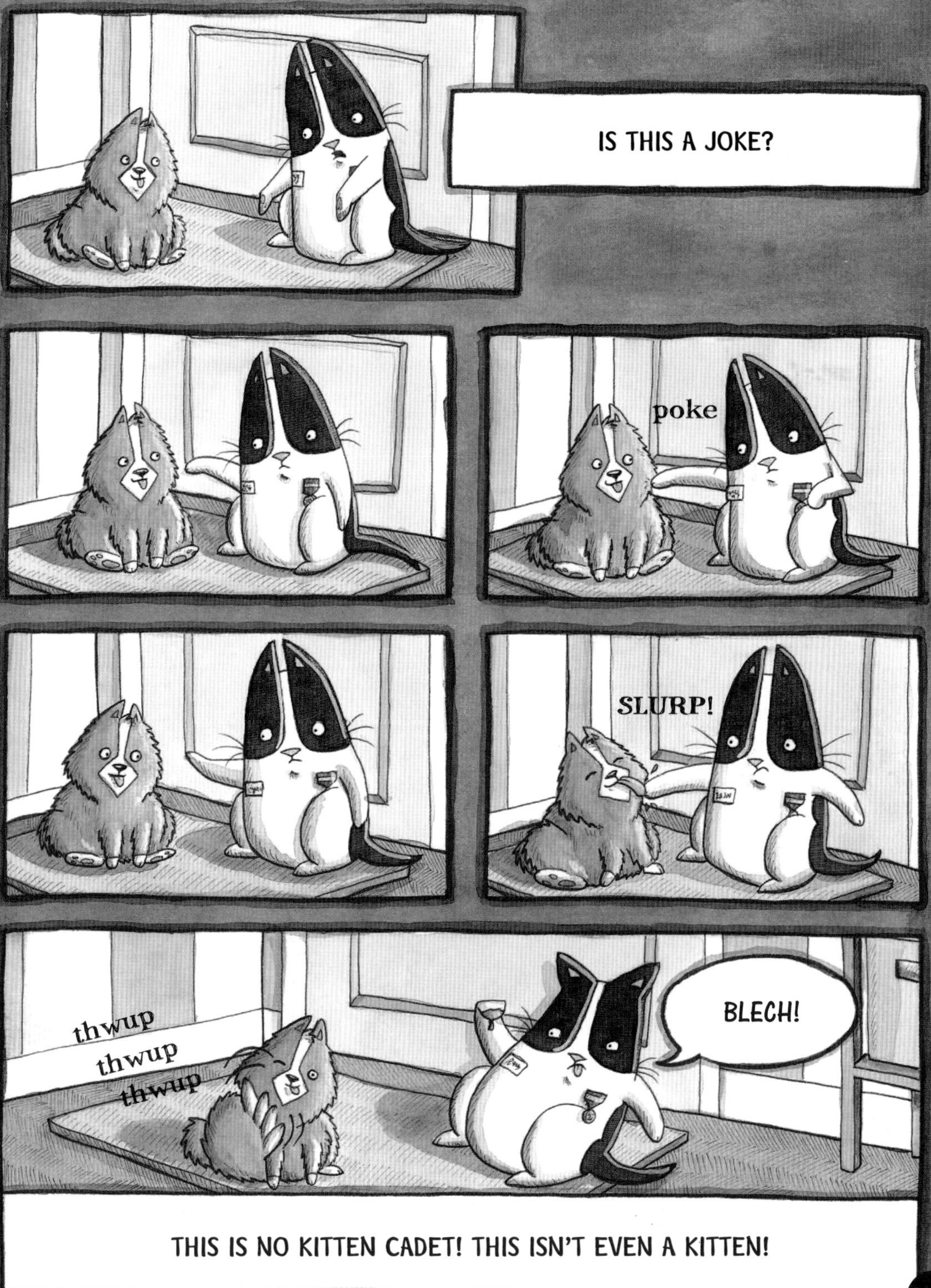

IS THIS A JOKE?
poke
SLURP!
thwup
thwup
thwup
BLECH!
THIS IS NO KITTEN CADET! THIS ISN'T EVEN A KITTEN!

BINKY HAS TO GET GRACIE!

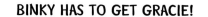

thrumpa thrump!

SHE'LL KNOW HOW TO FIX THIS.

scrish scroosh

smoosh

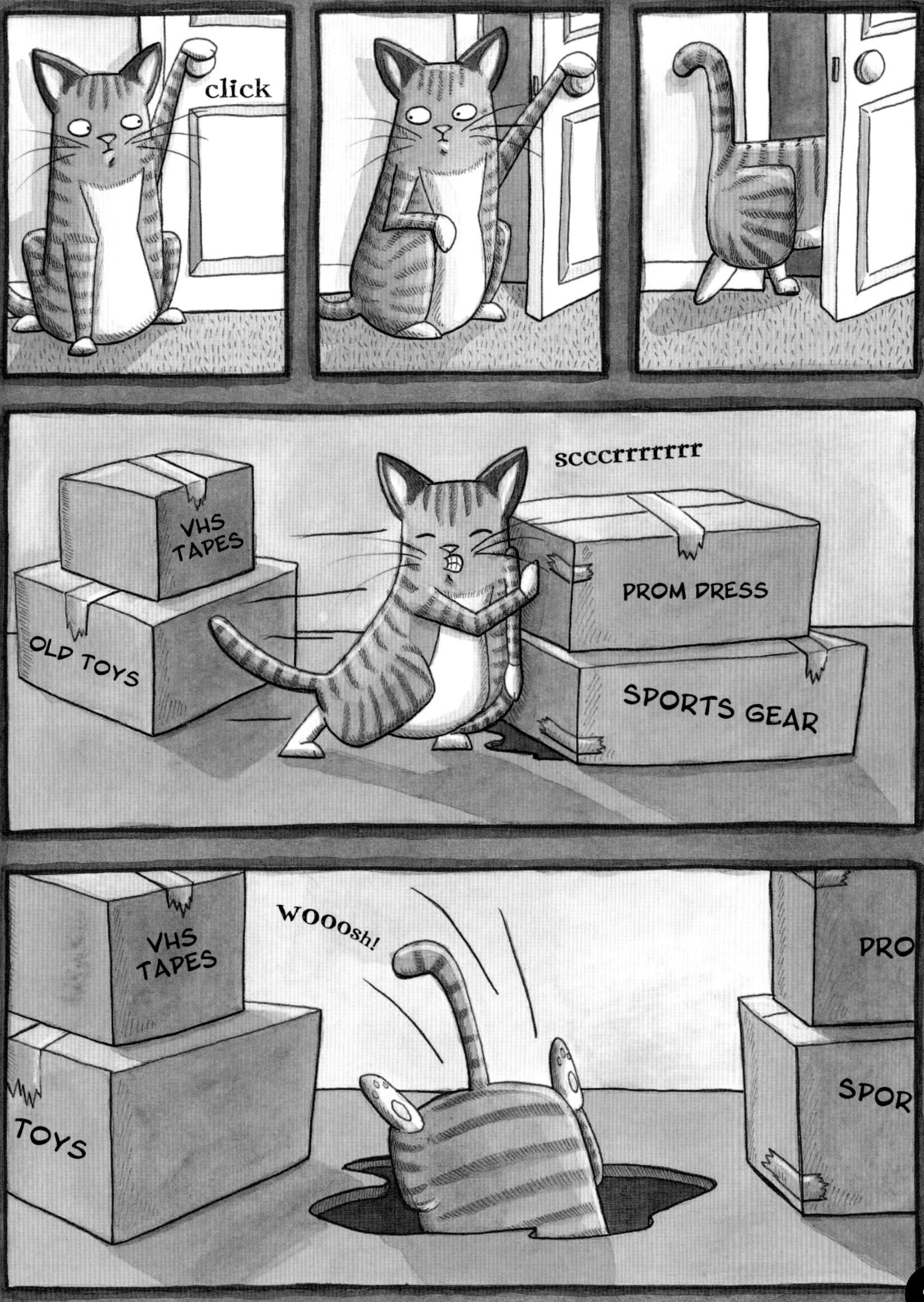
click
scccrrrrrrr
VHS TAPES
OLD TOYS
PROM DRESS
SPORTS GEAR
WOOOsh!
VHS TAPES
TOYS
PRO
SPOR

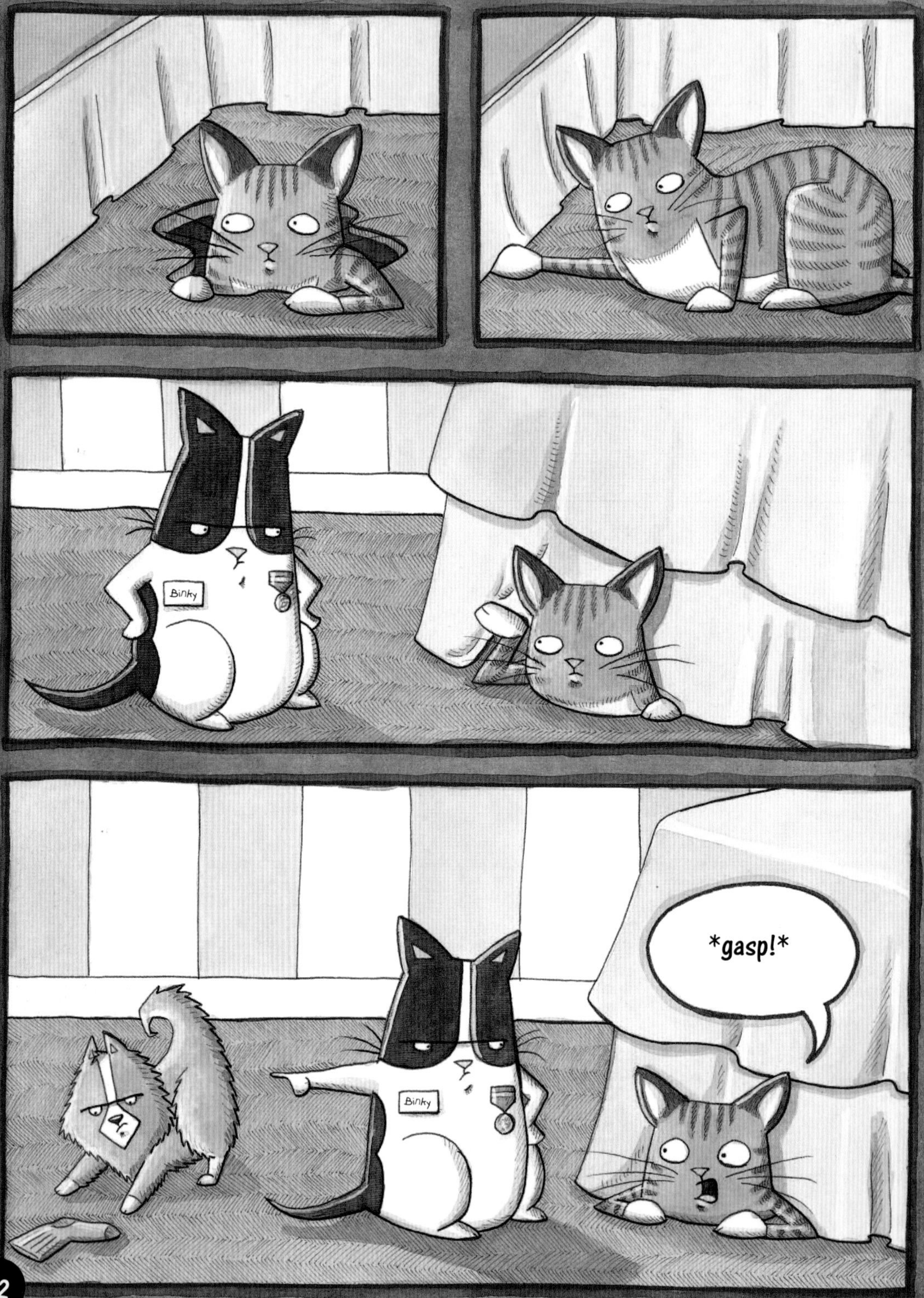

Binky
Binky
gasp!

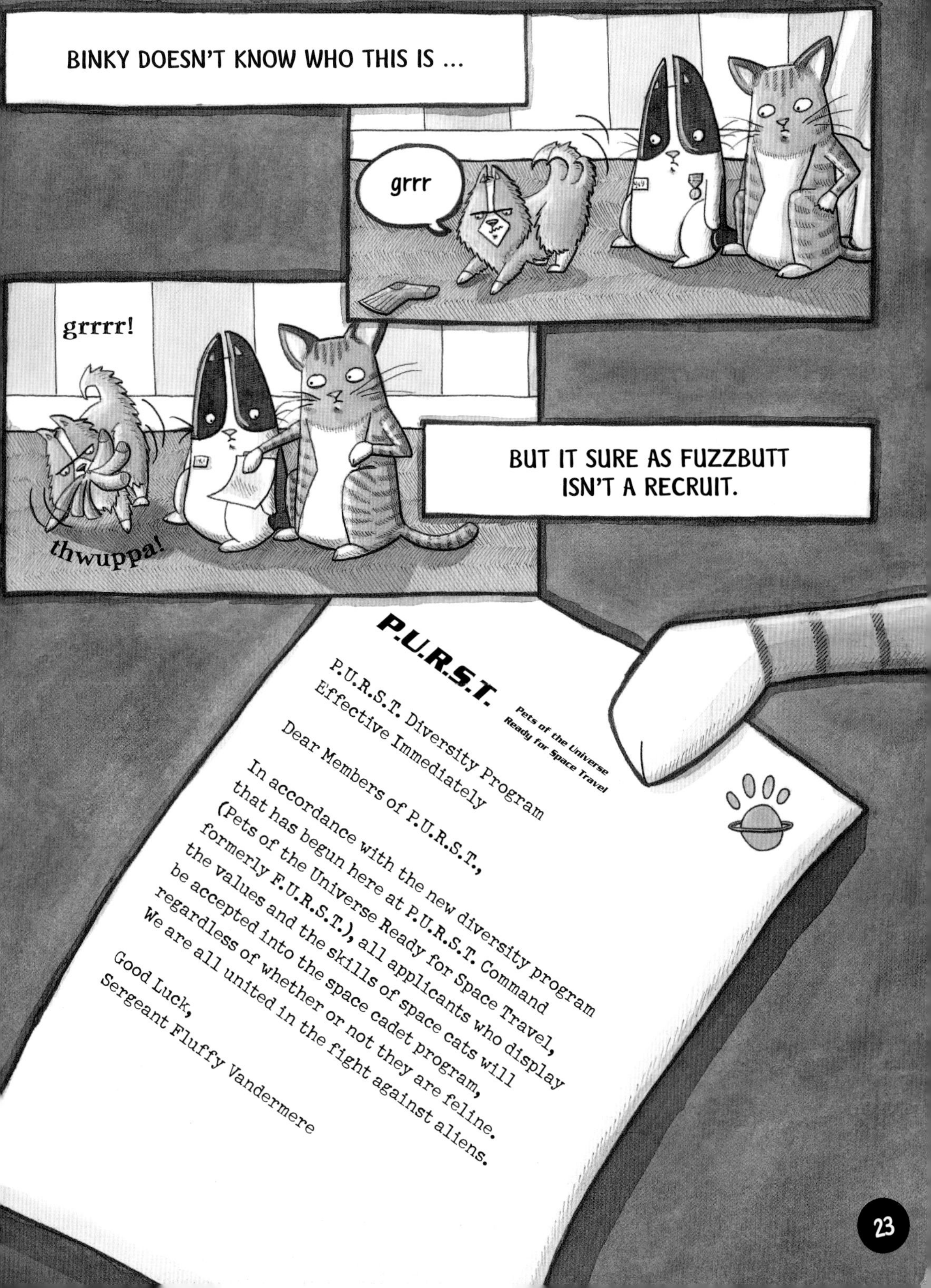
BINKY DOESN'T KNOW WHO THIS IS ...
grrr
grrrr!
thwuppa!
BUT IT SURE AS FUZZBUTT ISN'T A RECRUIT.
P.U.R.S.T.
Pets of the Universe Ready for Space Travel
P.U.R.S.T. Diversity Program
Effective Immediately
Dear Members of P.U.R.S.T.,
In accordance with the new diversity program that has begun here at P.U.R.S.T. Command (Pets of the Universe Ready for Space Travel, formerly F.U.R.S.T.), all applicants who display the values and the skills of space cats will be accepted into the space cadet program, regardless of whether or not they are feline. We are all united in the fight against aliens.
Good Luck,
Sergeant Fluffy Vandermere

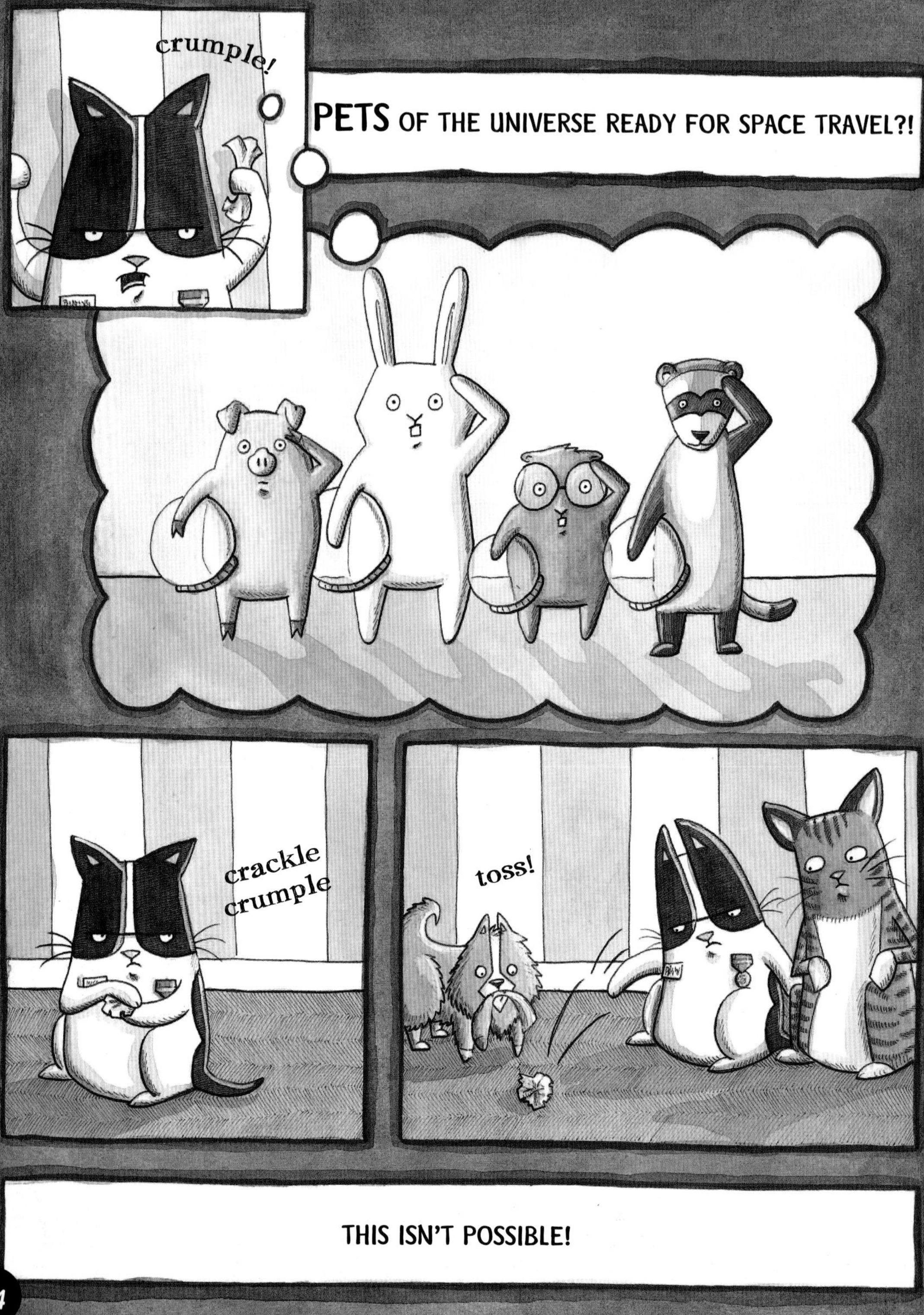
crumple!
PETS OF THE UNIVERSE READY FOR SPACE TRAVEL?!
crackle
crumple
toss!
THIS ISN'T POSSIBLE!

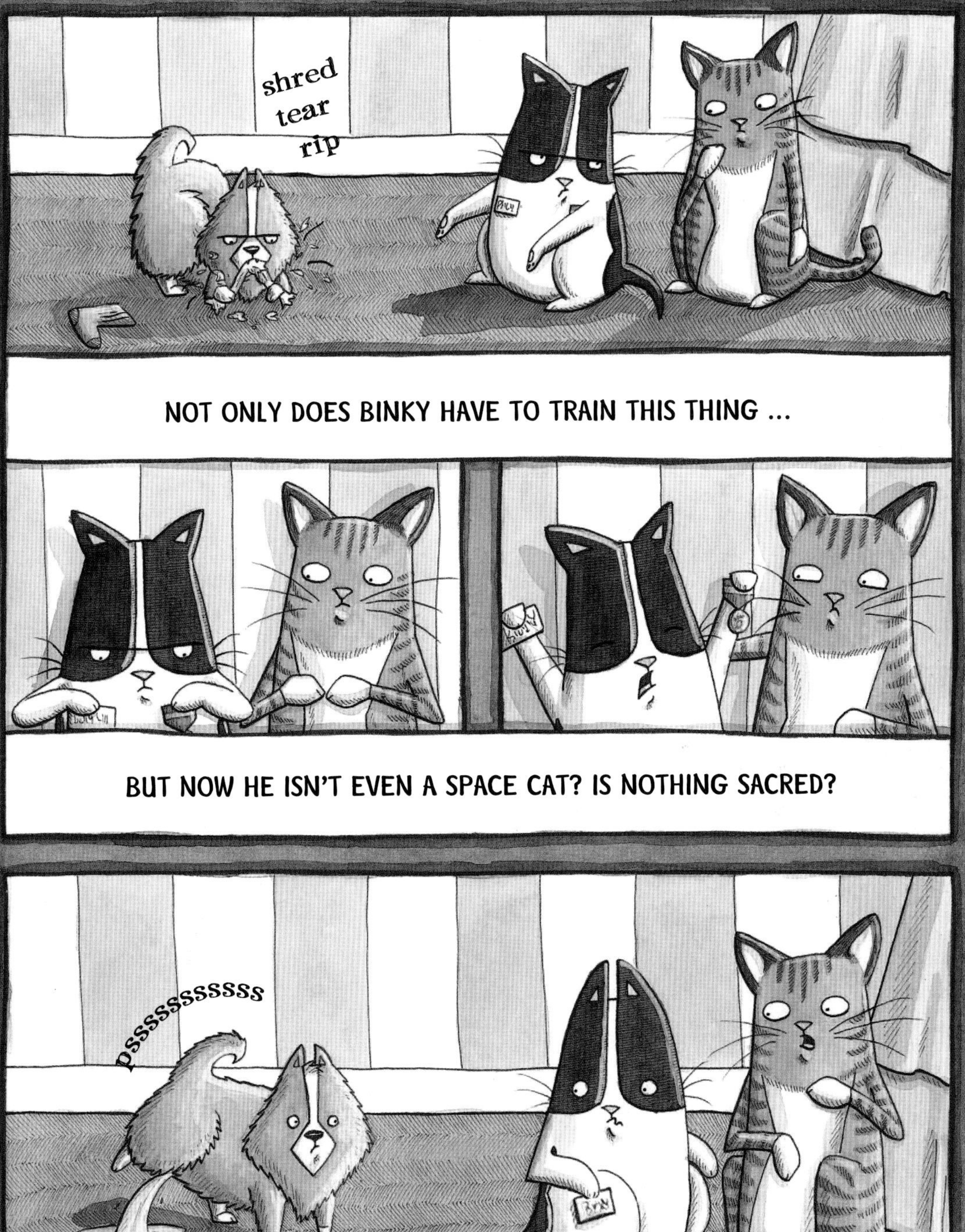
shred
tear
rip
NOT ONLY DOES BINKY HAVE TO TRAIN THIS THING ...
BUT NOW HE ISN'T EVEN A SPACE CAT? IS NOTHING SACRED?
psssssssssss

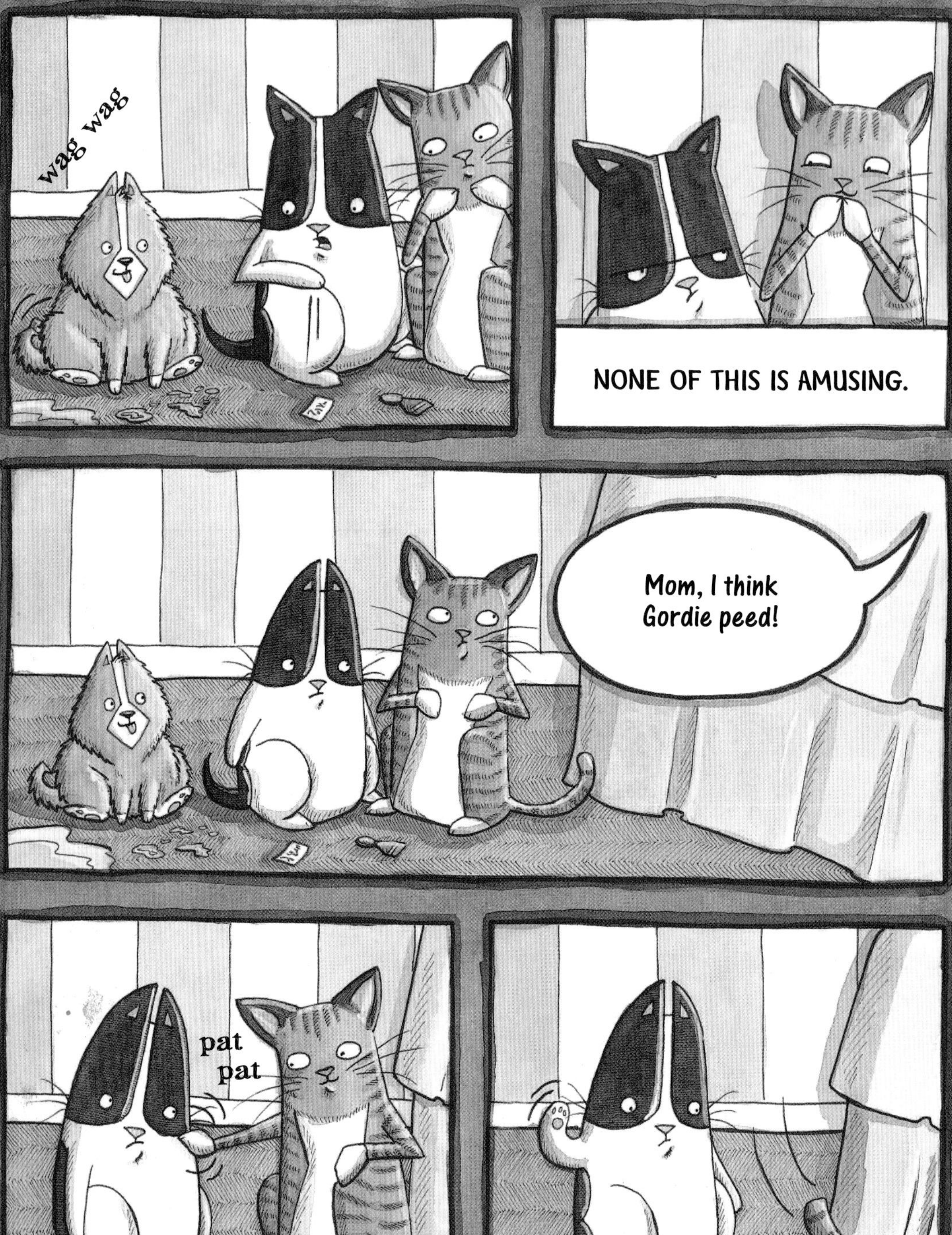
wag wag
NONE OF THIS IS AMUSING.
Mom, I think Gordie peed!
pat pat

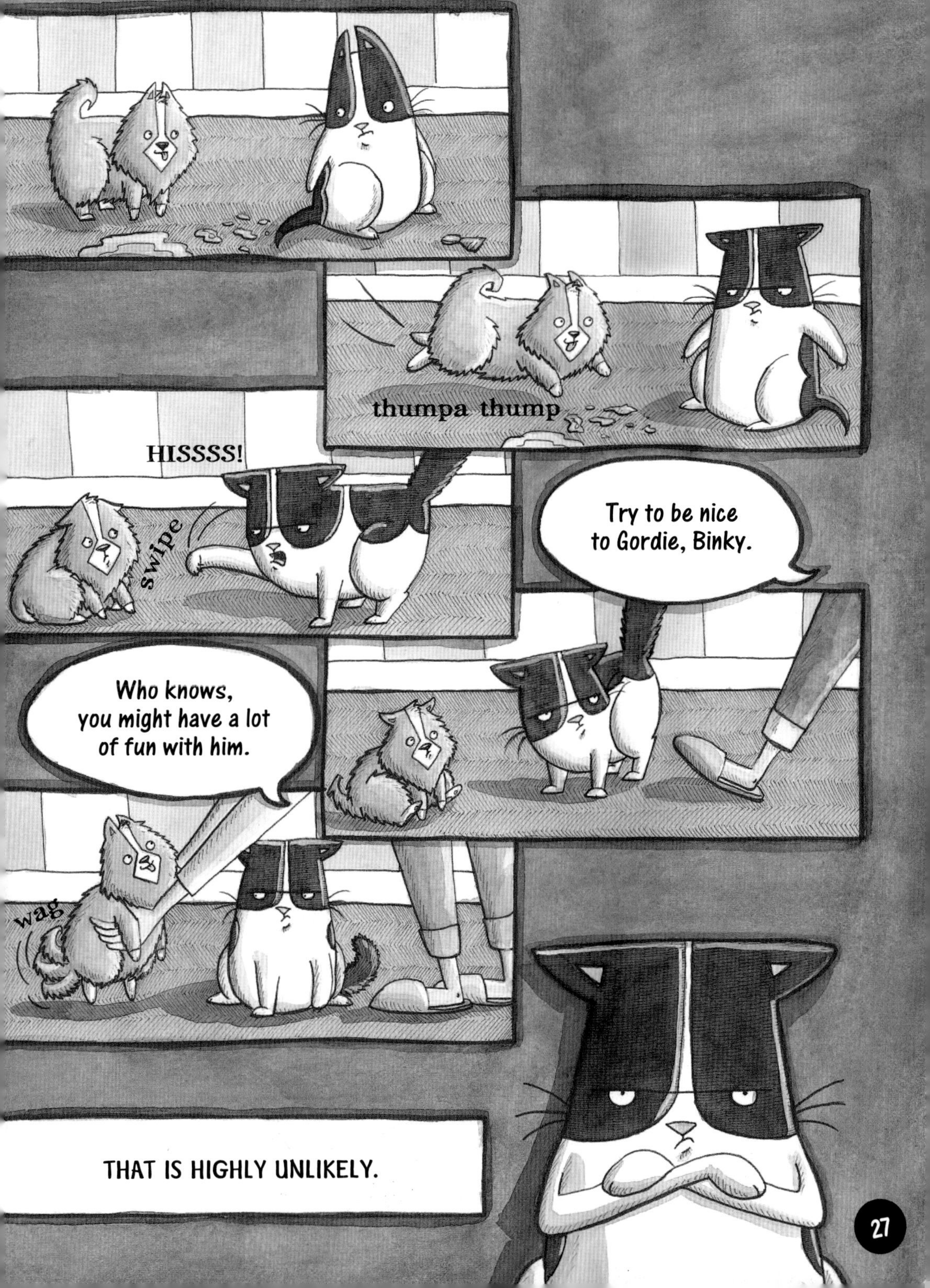

thumpa thump
HISSSS!
swipe
Try to be nice to Gordie, Binky.
Who knows, you might have a lot of fun with him.
wag
THAT IS HIGHLY UNLIKELY.

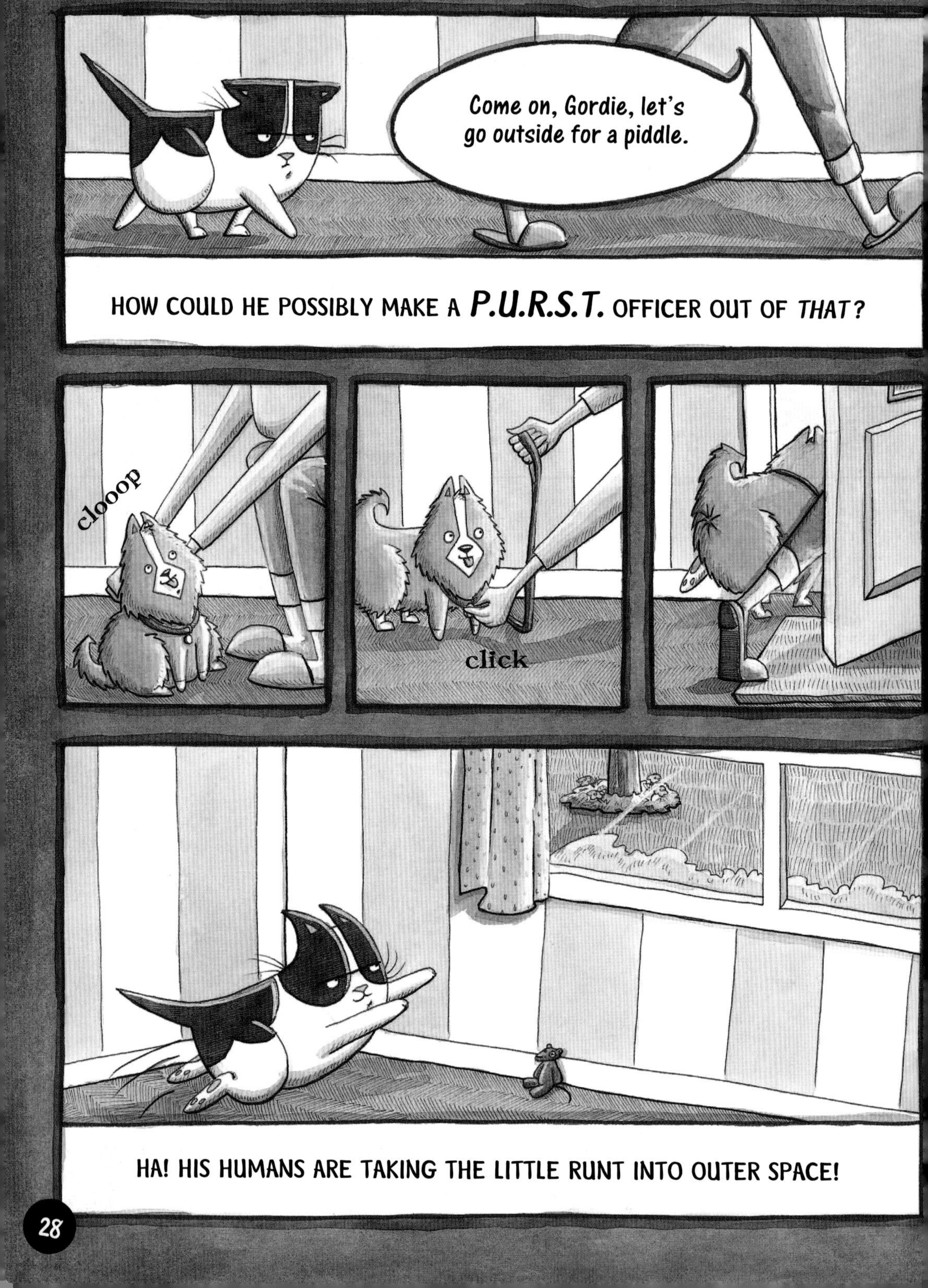

Come on, Gordie, let's go outside for a piddle.
HOW COULD HE POSSIBLY MAKE A P.U.R.S.T. OFFICER OUT OF THAT?
clooop
click
HA! HIS HUMANS ARE TAKING THE LITTLE RUNT INTO OUTER SPACE!

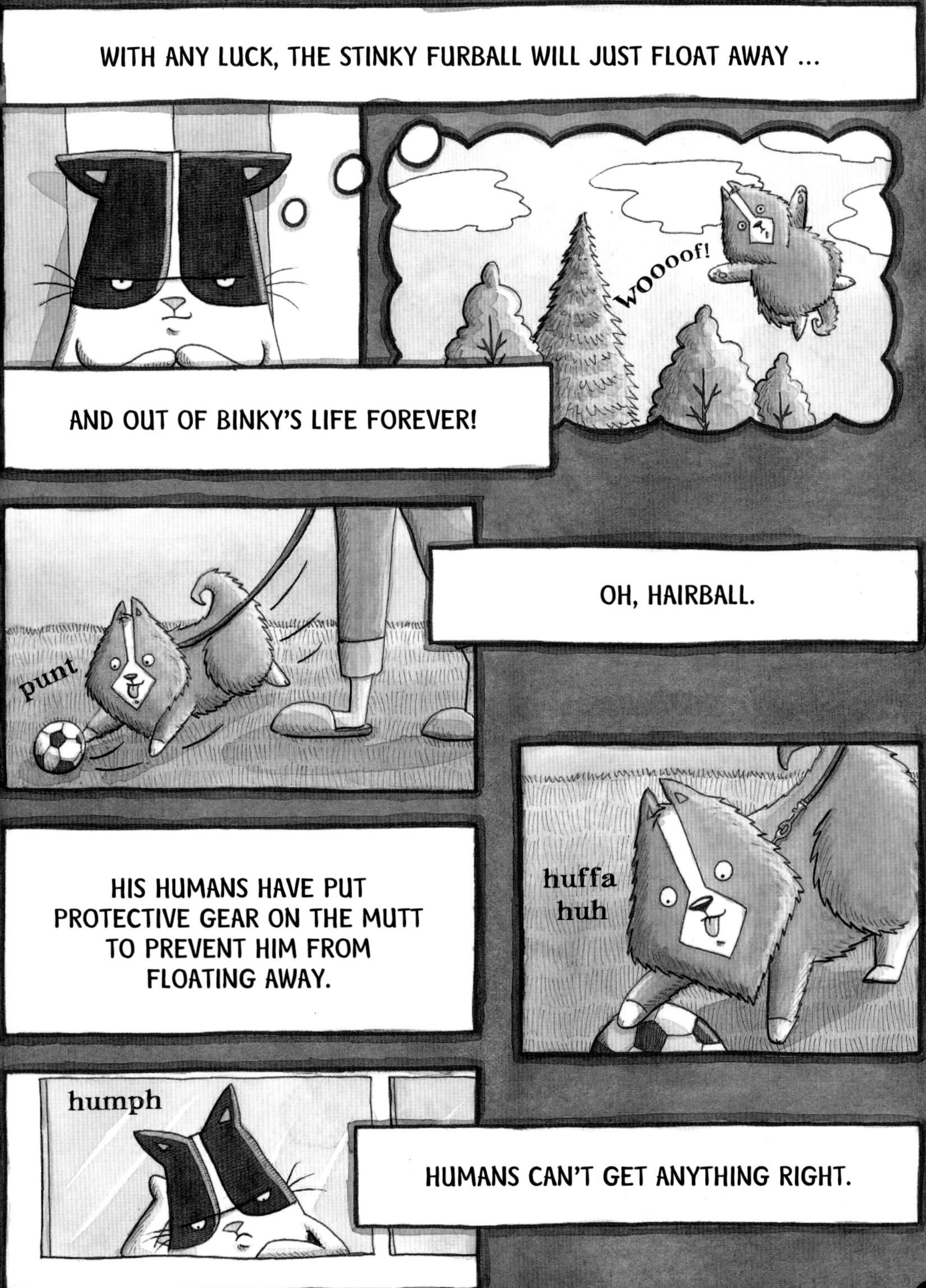
WITH ANY LUCK, THE STINKY FURBALL WILL JUST FLOAT AWAY ...
woooof!
AND OUT OF BINKY'S LIFE FOREVER!
punt
OH, HAIRBALL.
HIS HUMANS HAVE PUT PROTECTIVE GEAR ON THE MUTT TO PREVENT HIM FROM FLOATING AWAY.
huffa huh
humph
HUMANS CAN'T GET ANYTHING RIGHT.

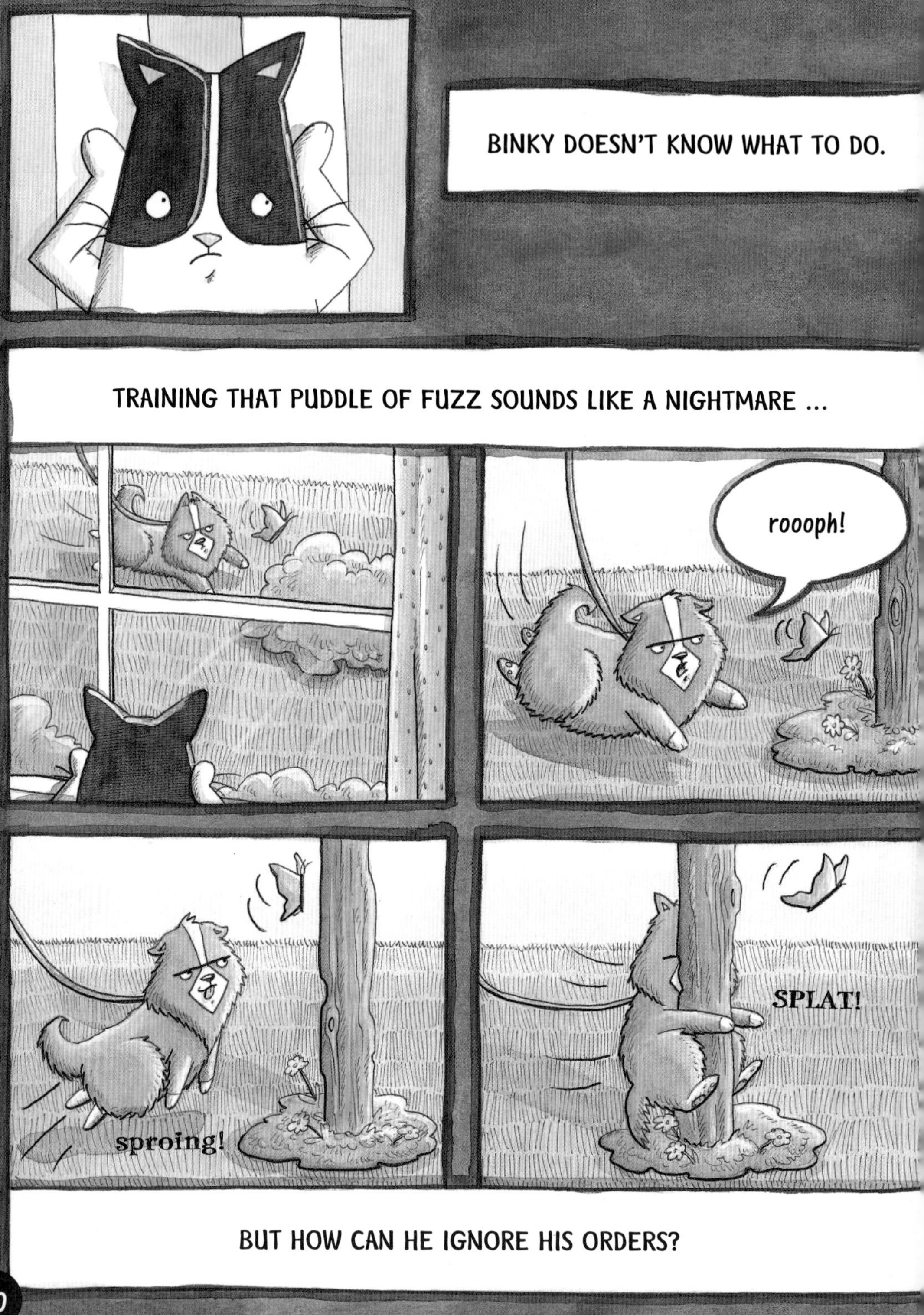
BINKY DOESN'T KNOW WHAT TO DO.
TRAINING THAT PUDDLE OF FUZZ SOUNDS LIKE A NIGHTMARE ...
roooph!
sproing!
SPLAT!
BUT HOW CAN HE IGNORE HIS ORDERS?

MAYBE IF HE TRIES TO MAKE AN OFFICER OUT OF A PUPPY ...

AND FAILS, THEN P.U.R.S.T. WILL SEE WHAT A SILLY IDEA THIS IS.

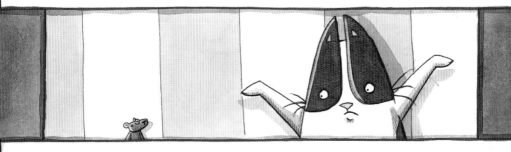

IF BINKY CAN'T TRAIN THIS CARPET-WETTER, THEN WHO CAN?

HE'LL GIVE IT A MONTH, AND IF GORDON HASN'T IMPROVED, OR AT LEAST BEEN HOUSE TRAINED, HE'LL SEND HIM BACK TO P.U.R.S.T. FOR GOOD!

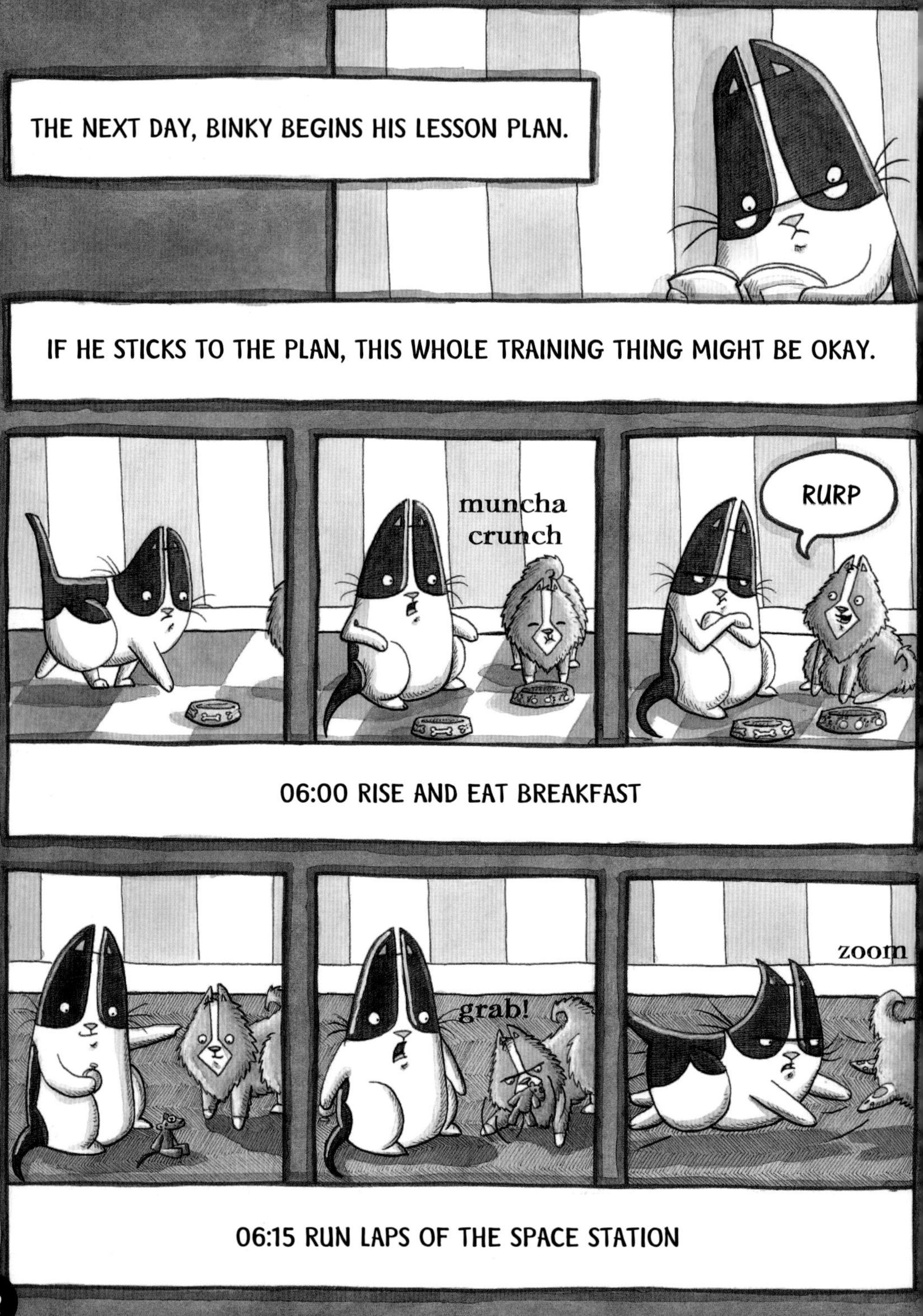
THE NEXT DAY, BINKY BEGINS HIS LESSON PLAN.
IF HE STICKS TO THE PLAN, THIS WHOLE TRAINING THING MIGHT BE OKAY.
muncha
crunch
RURP
06:00 RISE AND EAT BREAKFAST
grab!
zoom
06:15 RUN LAPS OF THE SPACE STATION

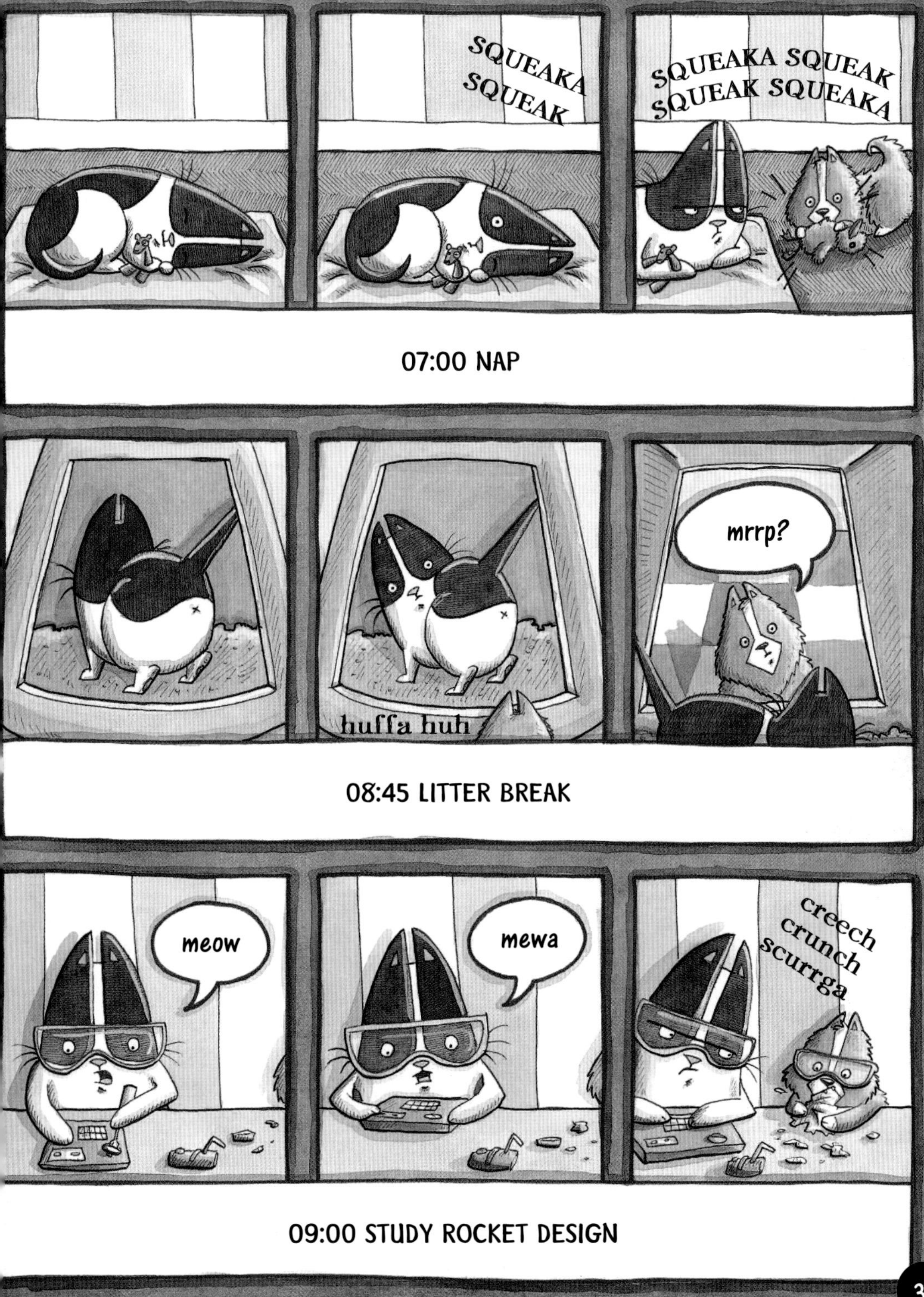
SQUEAKA SQUEAK
SQUEAKA SQUEAK SQUEAK SQUEAKA
07:00 NAP
huffa huh
mrrp?
08:45 LITTER BREAK
meow
mewa
creech crunch scurrga
09:00 STUDY ROCKET DESIGN

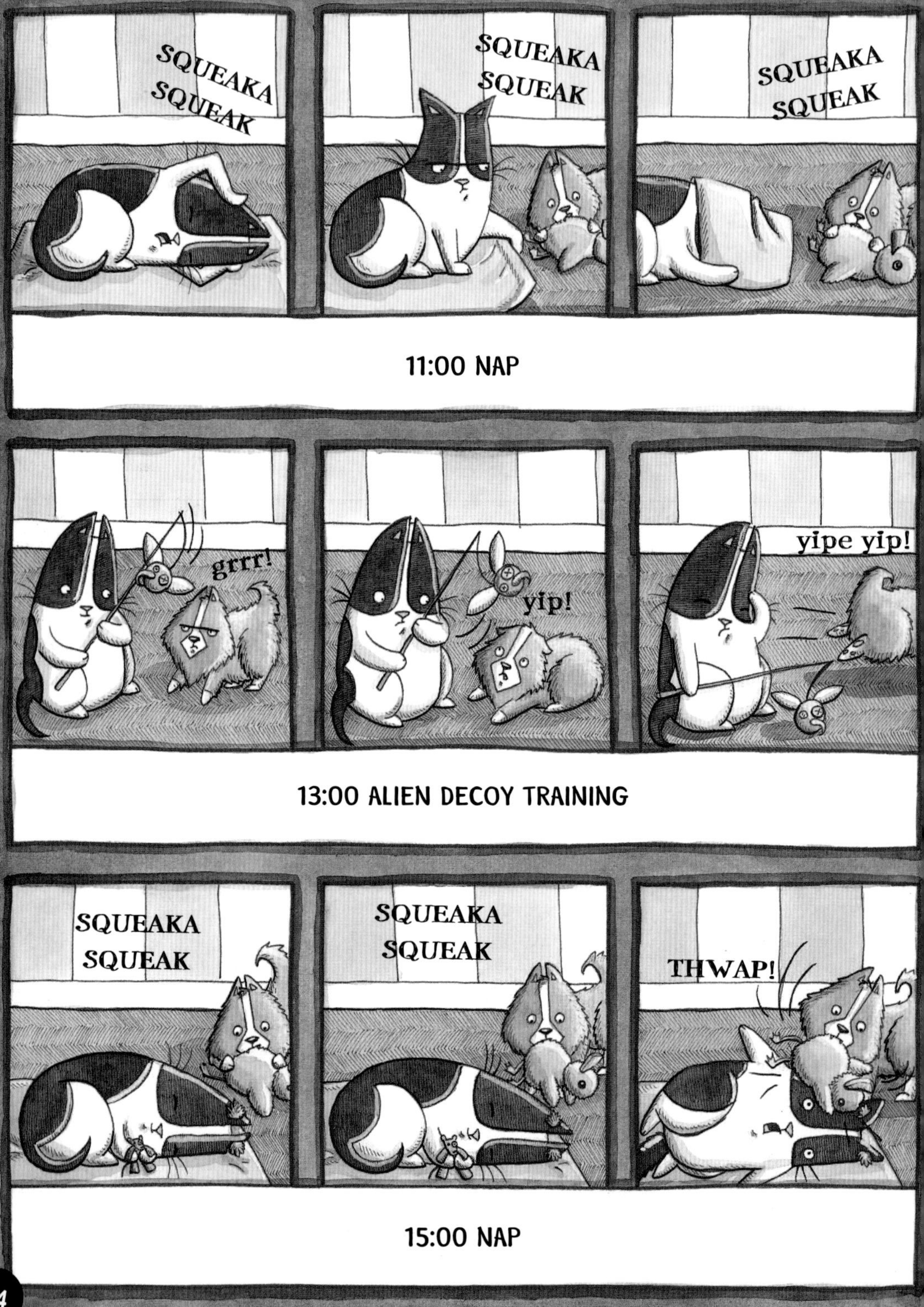
SQUEAKA SQUEAK
SQUEAKA SQUEAK
SQUEAKA SQUEAK
11:00 NAP
grrr!
yip!
yipe yip!
13:00 ALIEN DECOY TRAINING
SQUEAKA SQUEAK
SQUEAKA SQUEAK
THWAP!
15:00 NAP

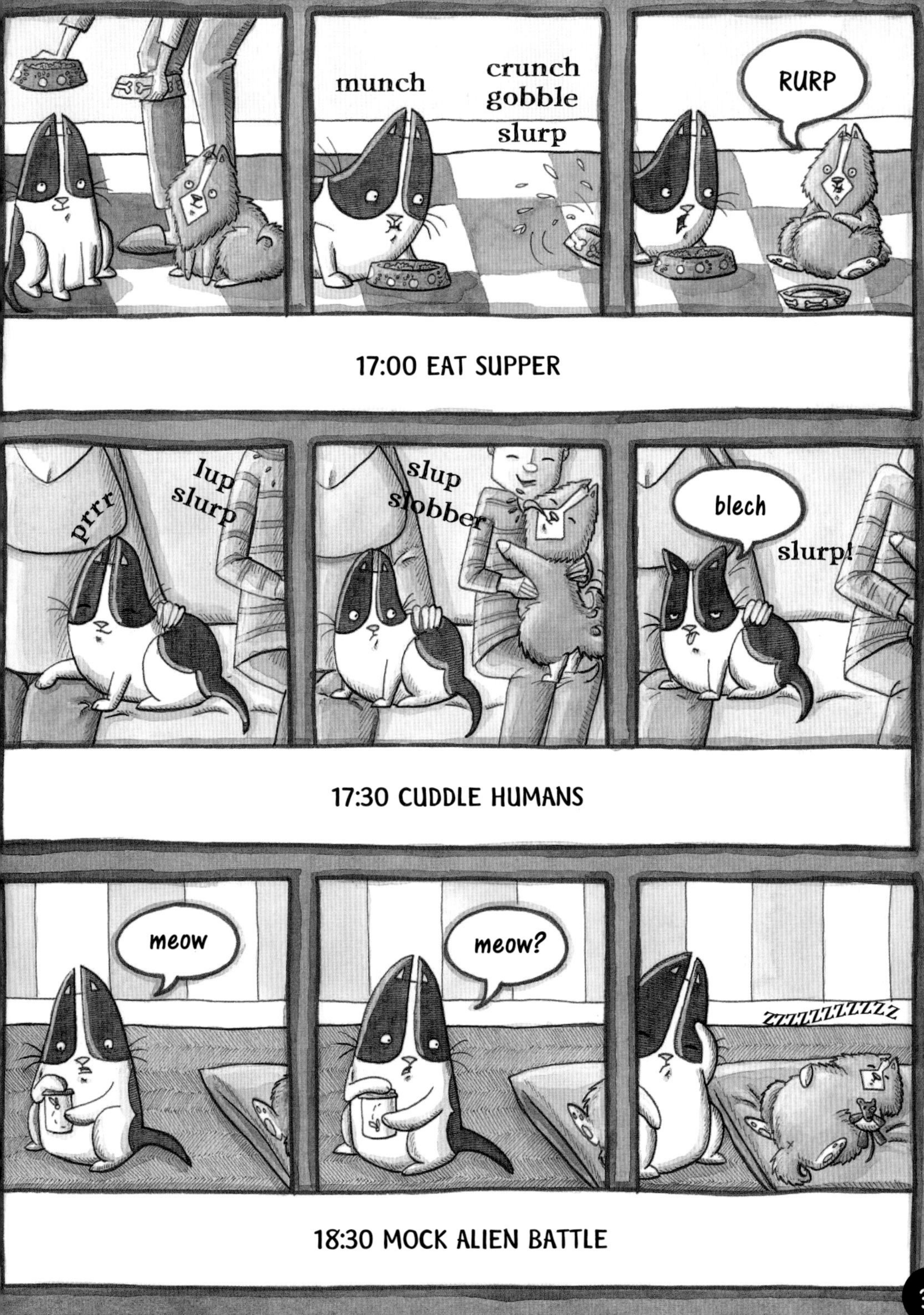
munch
crunch
gobble
slurp
RURP
17:00 EAT SUPPER
prrr
lup
slurp
slup
slobber
blech
slurp!
17:30 CUDDLE HUMANS
meow
meow?
18:30 MOCK ALIEN BATTLE

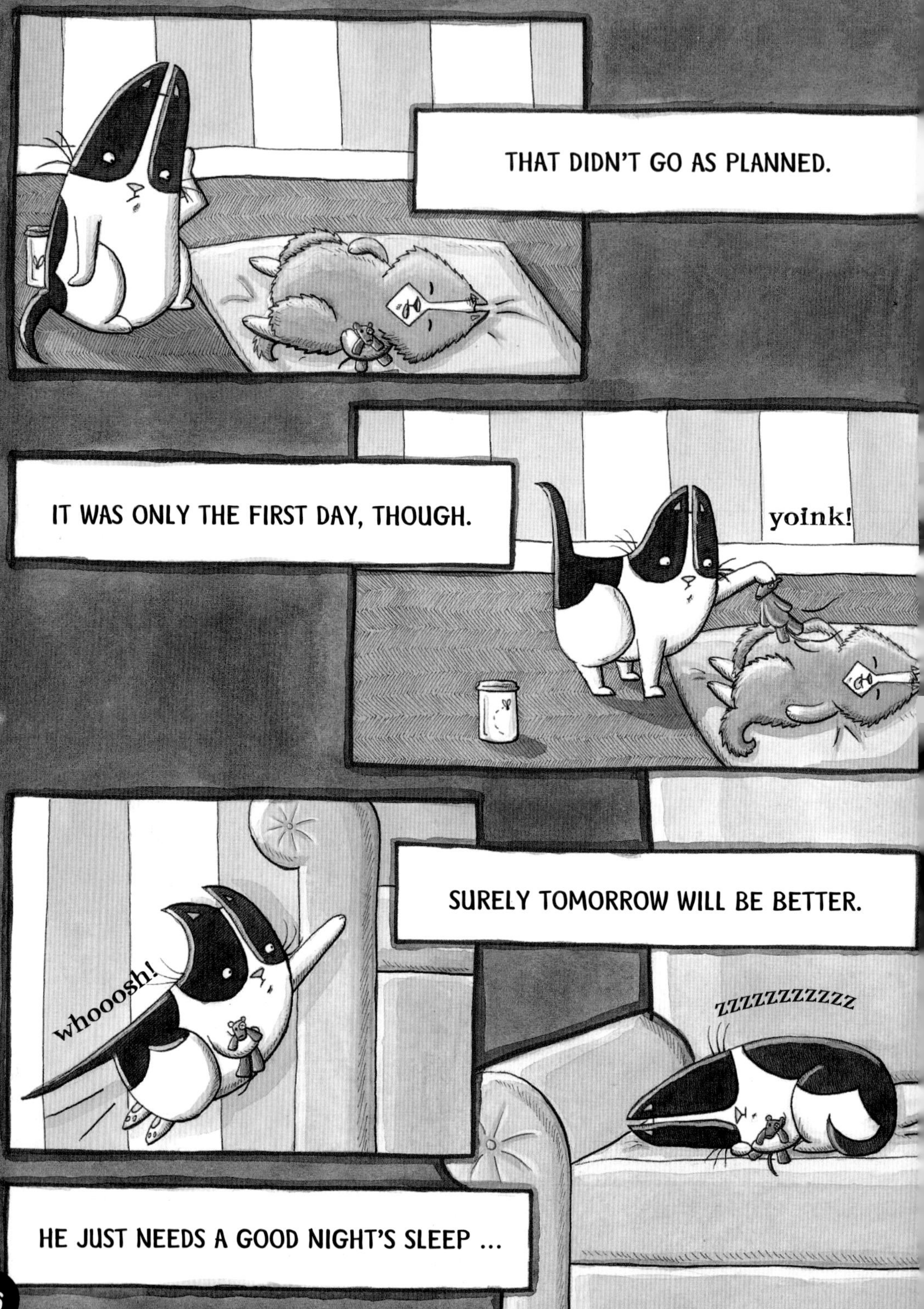
THAT DIDN'T GO AS PLANNED.
IT WAS ONLY THE FIRST DAY, THOUGH.
yoink!
SURELY TOMORROW WILL BE BETTER.
whoooosh!
HE JUST NEEDS A GOOD NIGHT'S SLEEP ...
ZZZZZZZZZZ

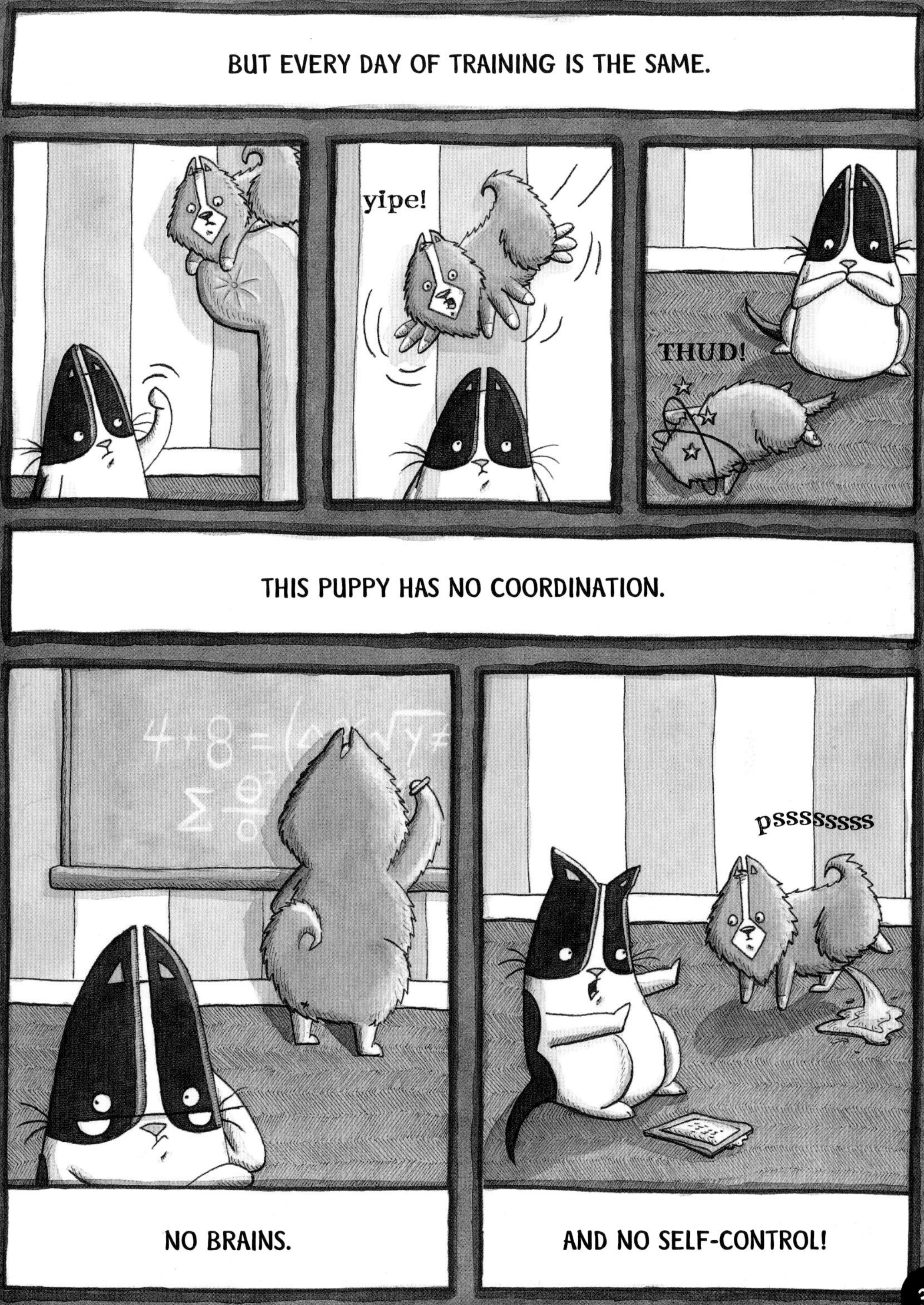
BUT EVERY DAY OF TRAINING IS THE SAME.
yipe!
THUD!
THIS PUPPY HAS NO COORDINATION.
NO BRAINS.
pssssssss
AND NO SELF-CONTROL!

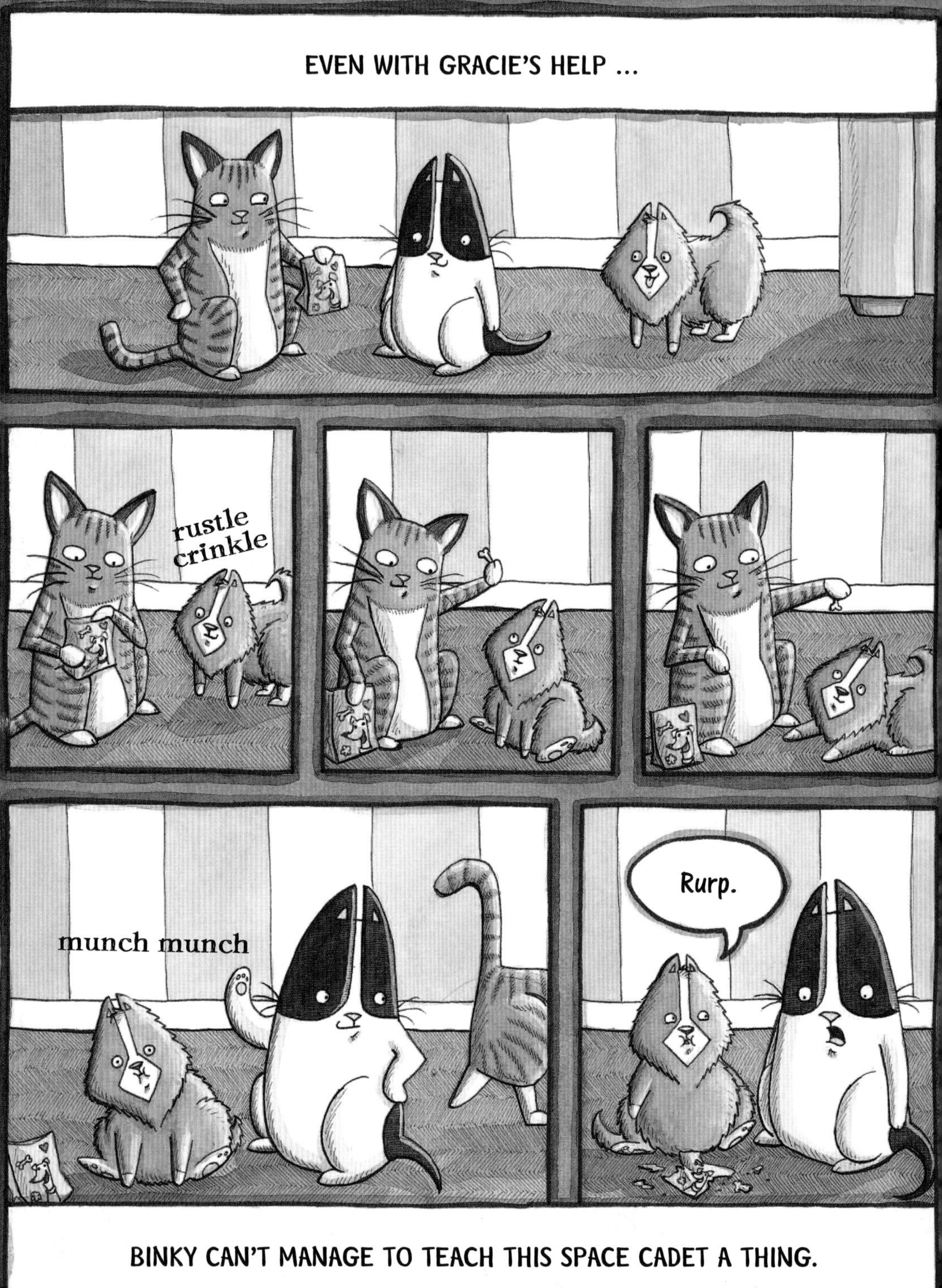

EVEN WITH GRACIE'S HELP ...
rustle crinkle
munch munch
Rurp.
BINKY CAN'T MANAGE TO TEACH THIS SPACE CADET A THING.

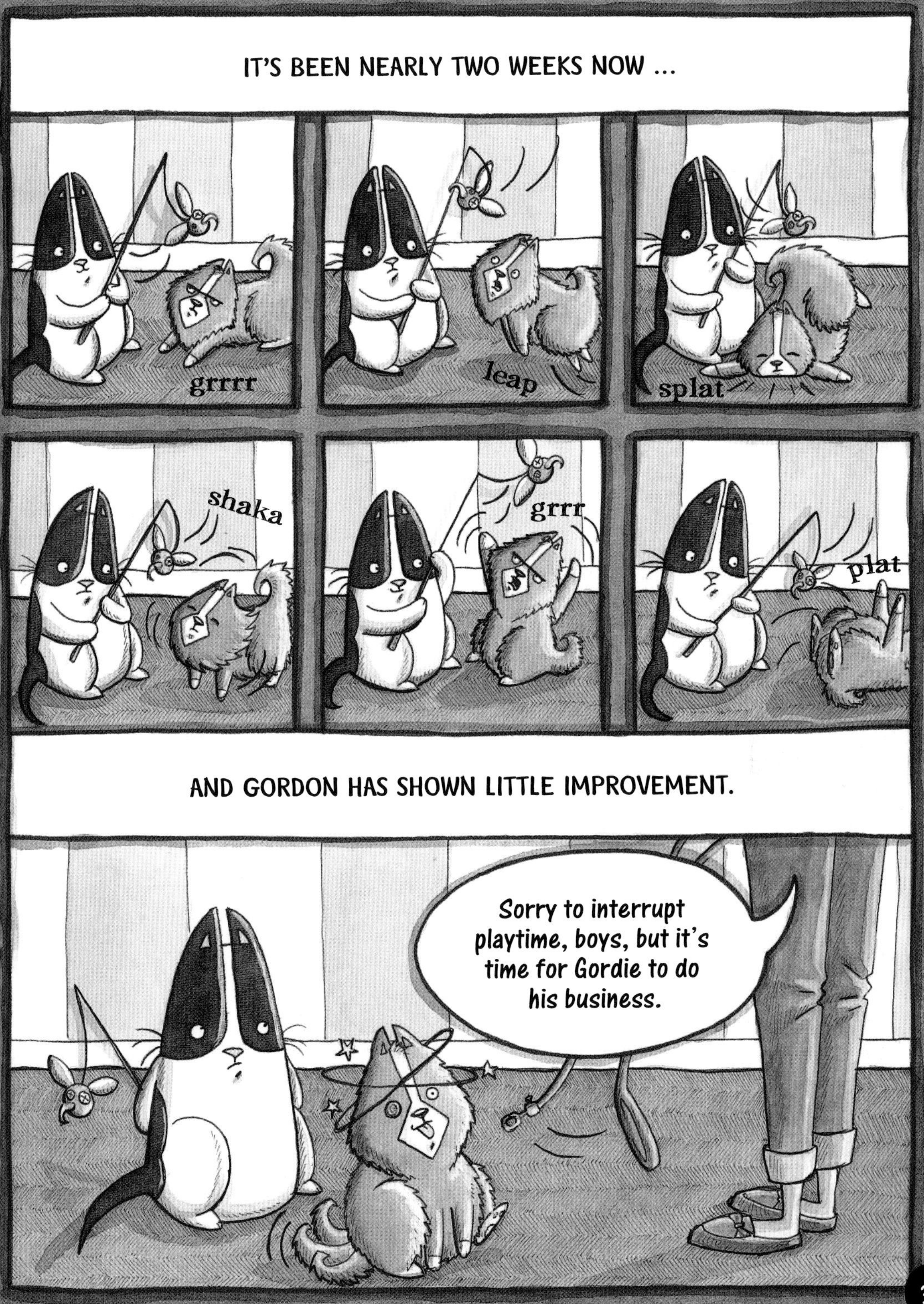
IT'S BEEN NEARLY TWO WEEKS NOW ...
grrrr
leap
splat
shaka
grrr
plat
AND GORDON HAS SHOWN LITTLE IMPROVEMENT.
Sorry to interrupt playtime, boys, but it's time for Gordie to do his business.

THIS IS USELESS.

A **DOG** CANNOT BE A SPACE CAT!

HE CAN'T EVEN USE THE LITTER BOX
LIKE A CIVILIZED ANIMAL!

WAIT A MINUTE!

THOSE ALIENS SURE ARE INTERESTED
IN GORDON'S BUSINESS.

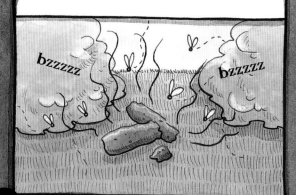

bzzzzz

bzzzzz

TOO INTERESTED.

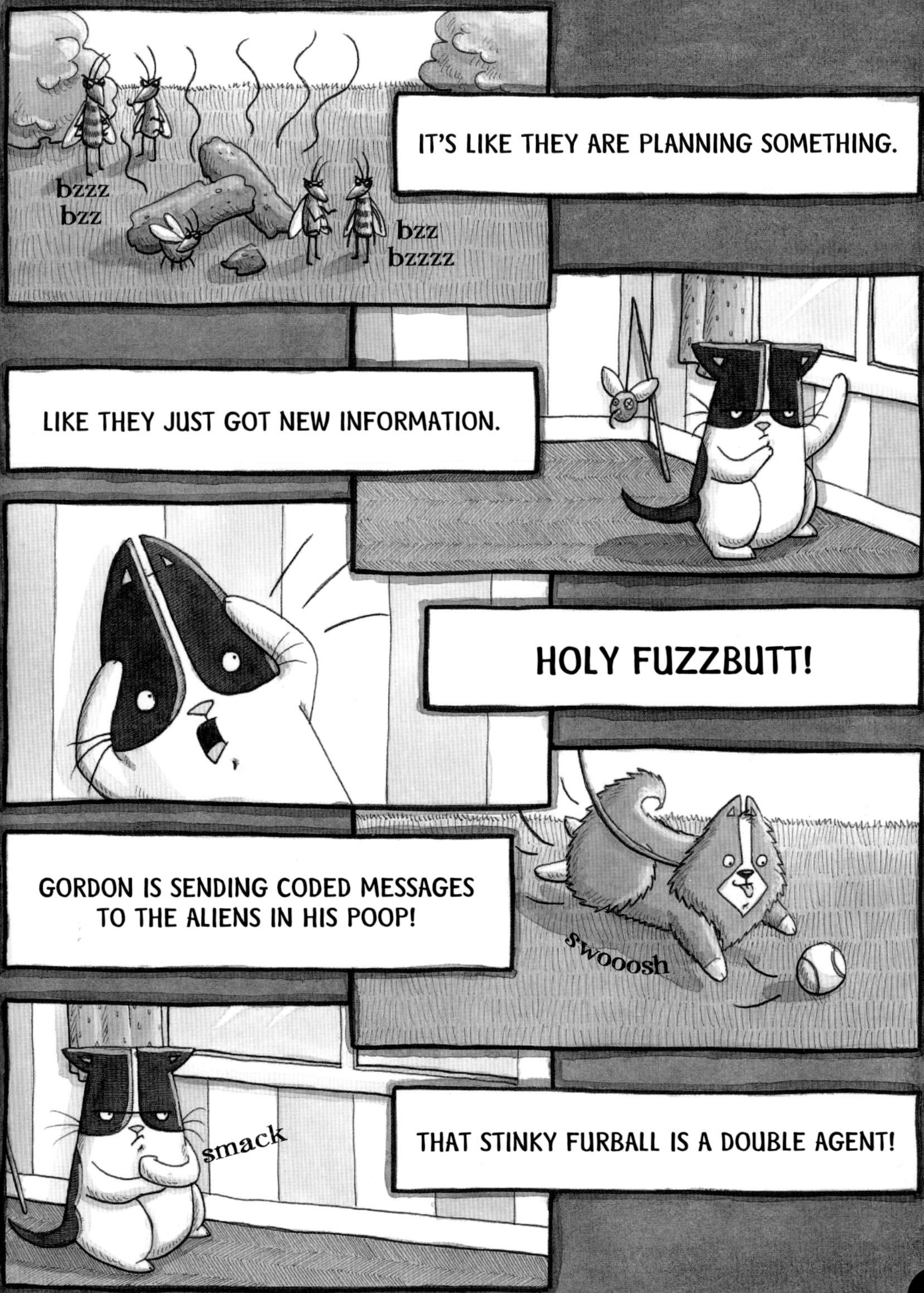
bzzz
bzz
bzz
bzzzz
IT'S LIKE THEY ARE PLANNING SOMETHING.
LIKE THEY JUST GOT NEW INFORMATION.
HOLY FUZZBUTT!
GORDON IS SENDING CODED MESSAGES TO THE ALIENS IN HIS POOP!
swooosh
THAT STINKY FURBALL IS A DOUBLE AGENT!
smack

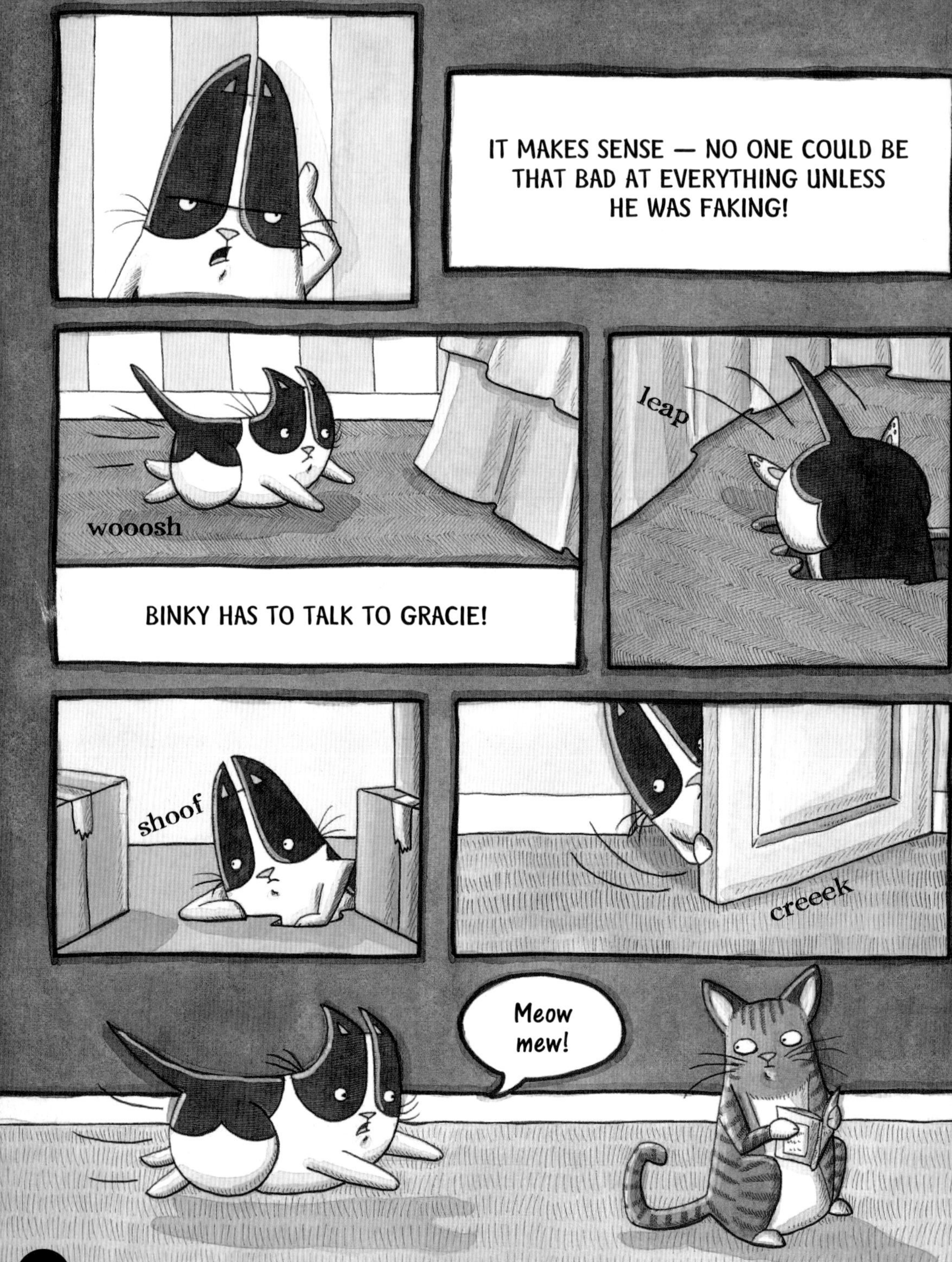

IT MAKES SENSE — NO ONE COULD BE THAT BAD AT EVERYTHING UNLESS HE WAS FAKING!
wooosh
BINKY HAS TO TALK TO GRACIE!
leap
shoof
creeek
Meow mew!

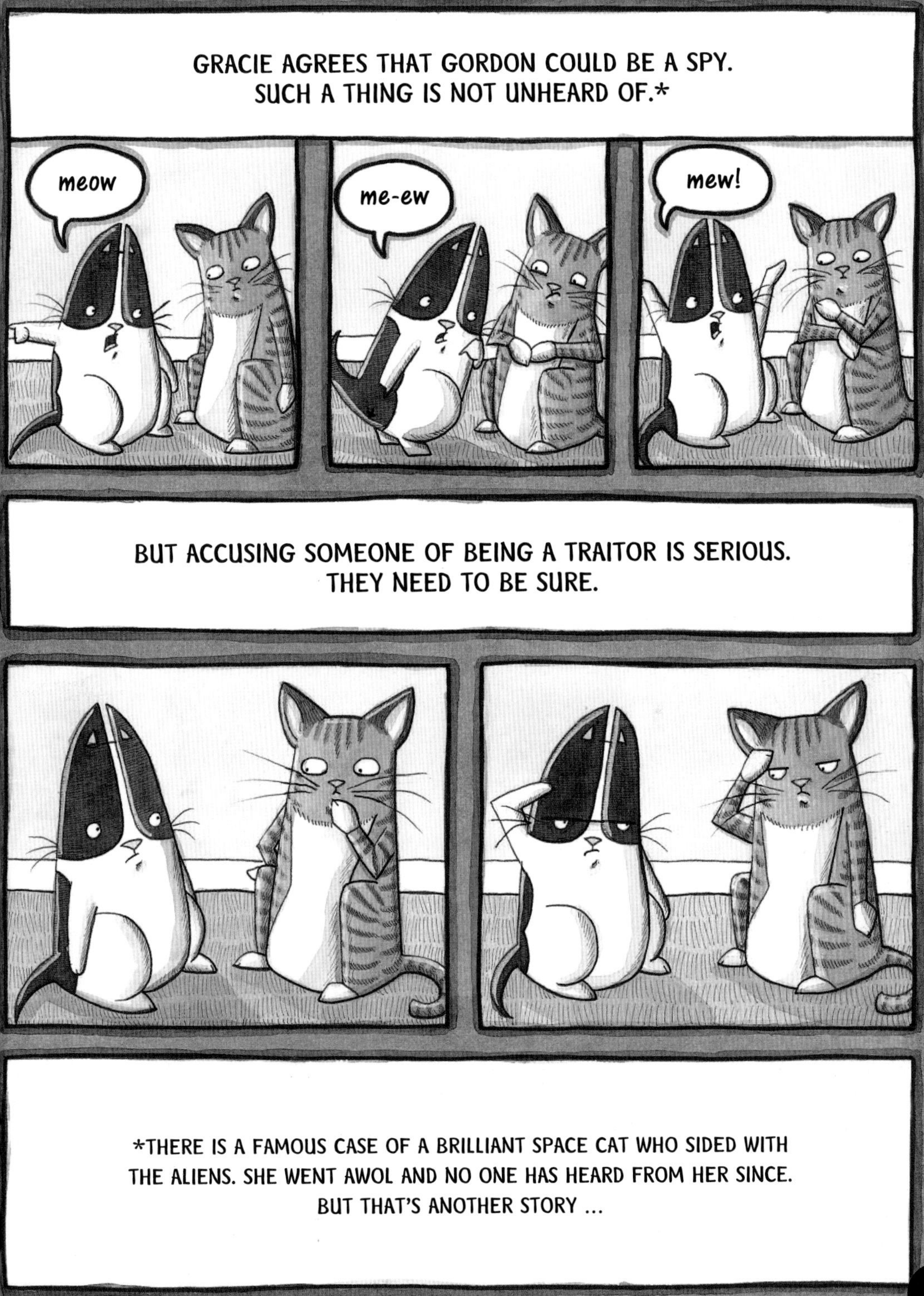
GRACIE AGREES THAT GORDON COULD BE A SPY.
SUCH A THING IS NOT UNHEARD OF.*
meow
me-ew
mew!
BUT ACCUSING SOMEONE OF BEING A TRAITOR IS SERIOUS.
THEY NEED TO BE SURE.
*THERE IS A FAMOUS CASE OF A BRILLIANT SPACE CAT WHO SIDED WITH THE ALIENS. SHE WENT AWOL AND NO ONE HAS HEARD FROM HER SINCE. BUT THAT'S ANOTHER STORY ...

woosh

GOOD THING BINKY IS A MASTER OF SURVEILLANCE.

ZIPPPPP!

smoosha
squish

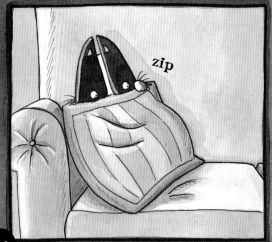
zip

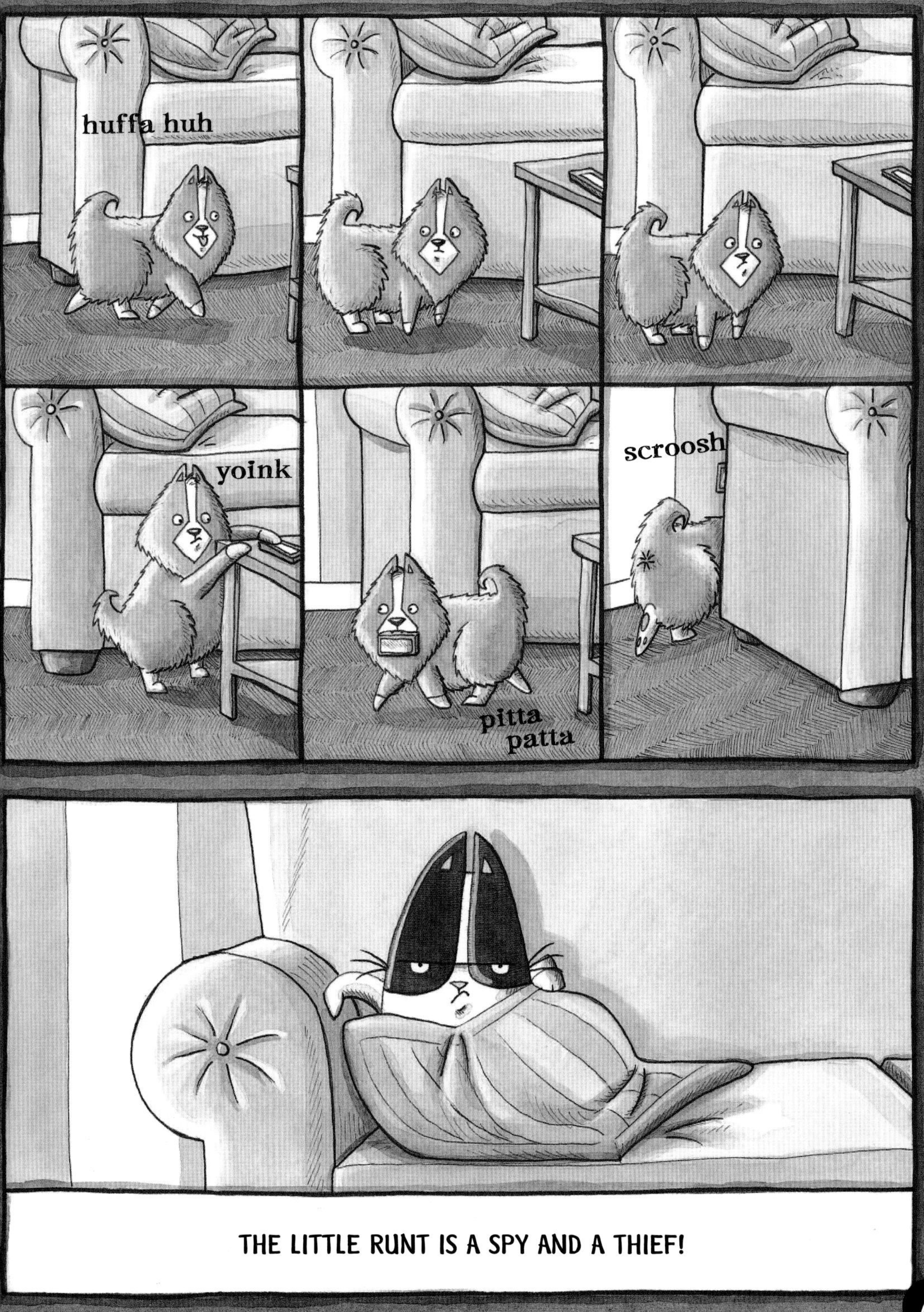
huffa huh
yoink
pitta patta
scroosh
THE LITTLE RUNT IS A SPY AND A THIEF!

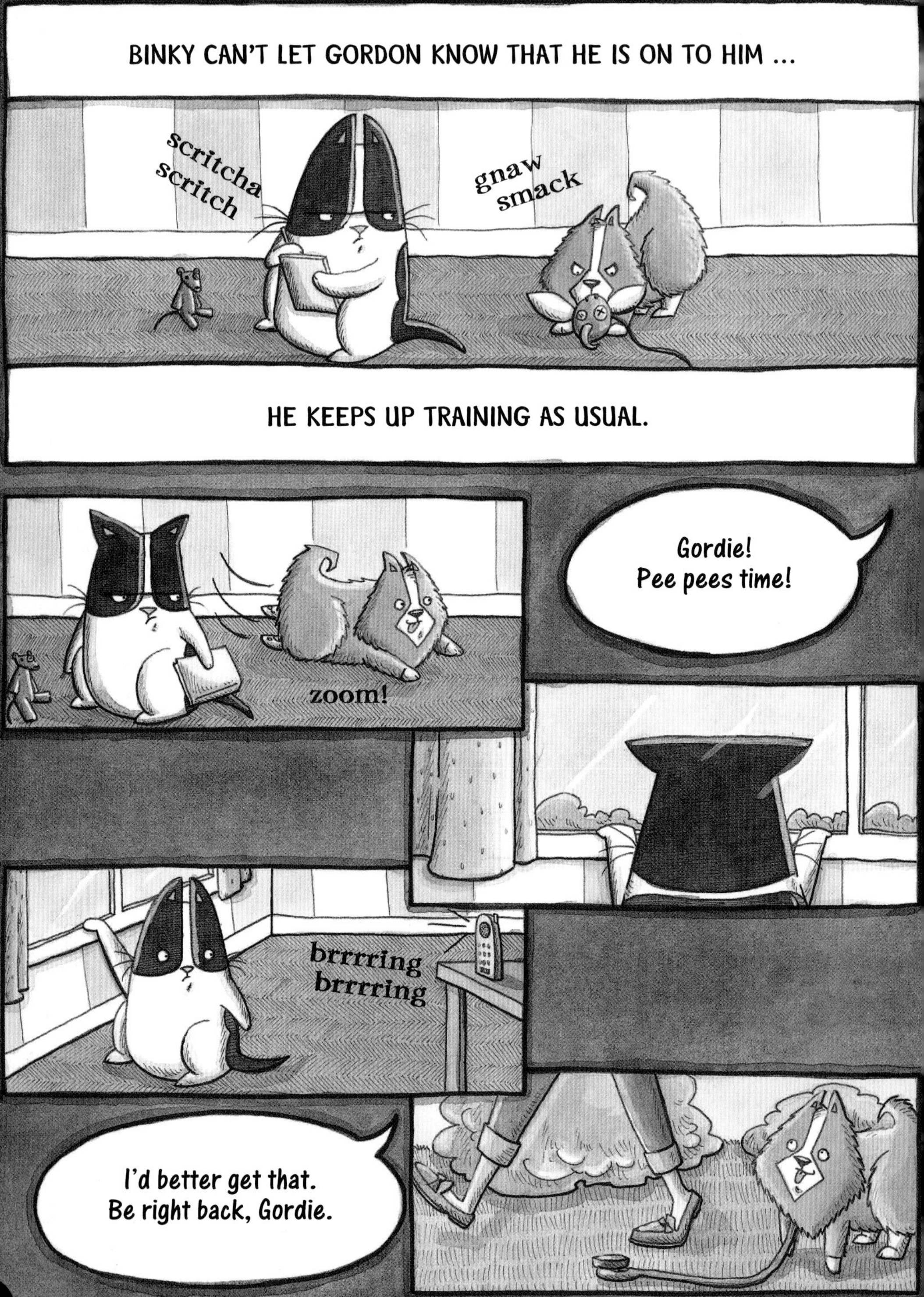
BINKY CAN'T LET GORDON KNOW THAT HE IS ON TO HIM ...
scritcha
scritch
gnaw
smack
HE KEEPS UP TRAINING AS USUAL.
zoom!
Gordie!
Pee pees time!
brrrring
brrrring
I'd better get that.
Be right back, Gordie.

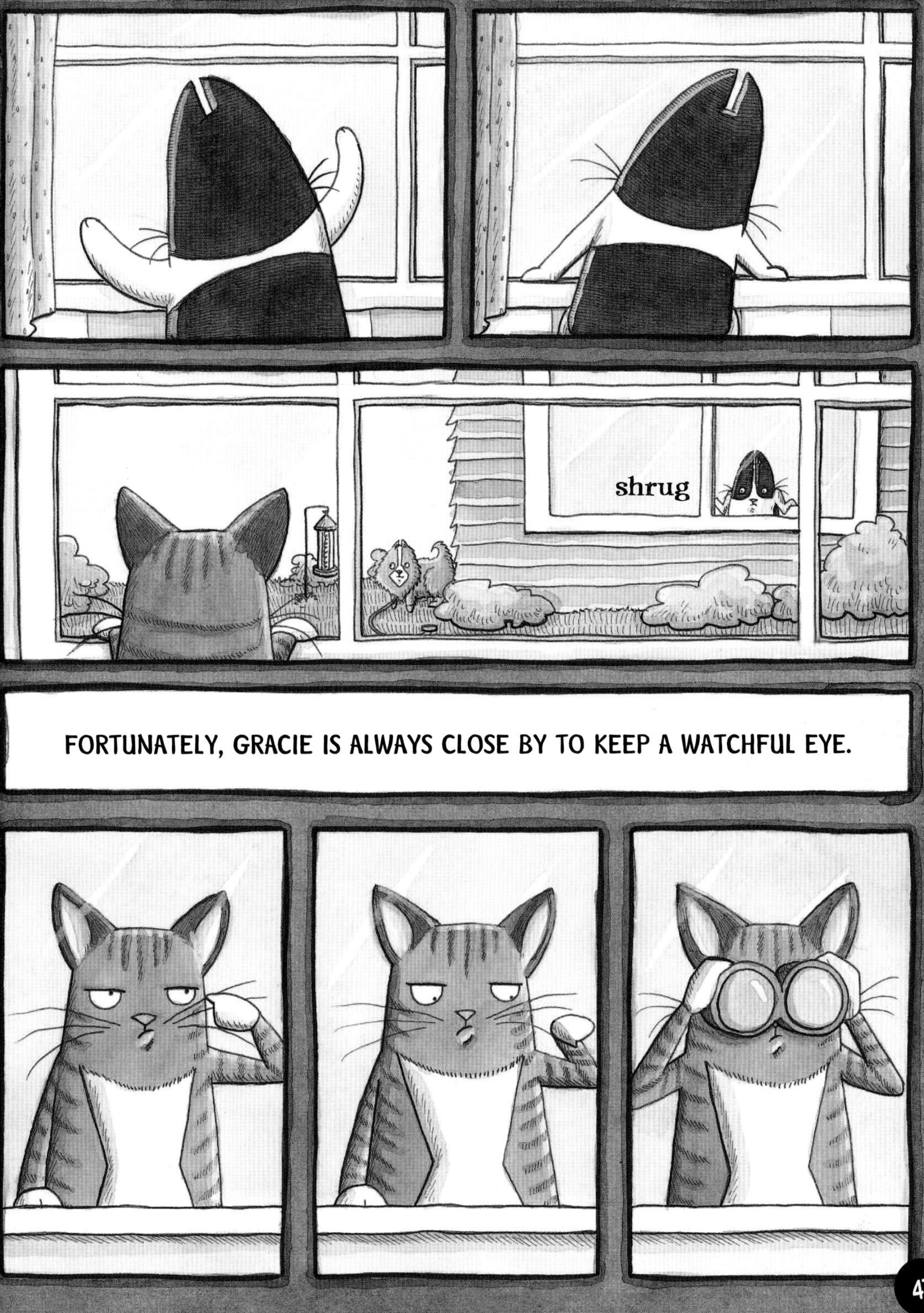
shrug
FORTUNATELY, GRACIE IS ALWAYS CLOSE BY TO KEEP A WATCHFUL EYE.

WHAT IS GORDON DOING WITH THAT ANTI-ALIEN DEVICE?

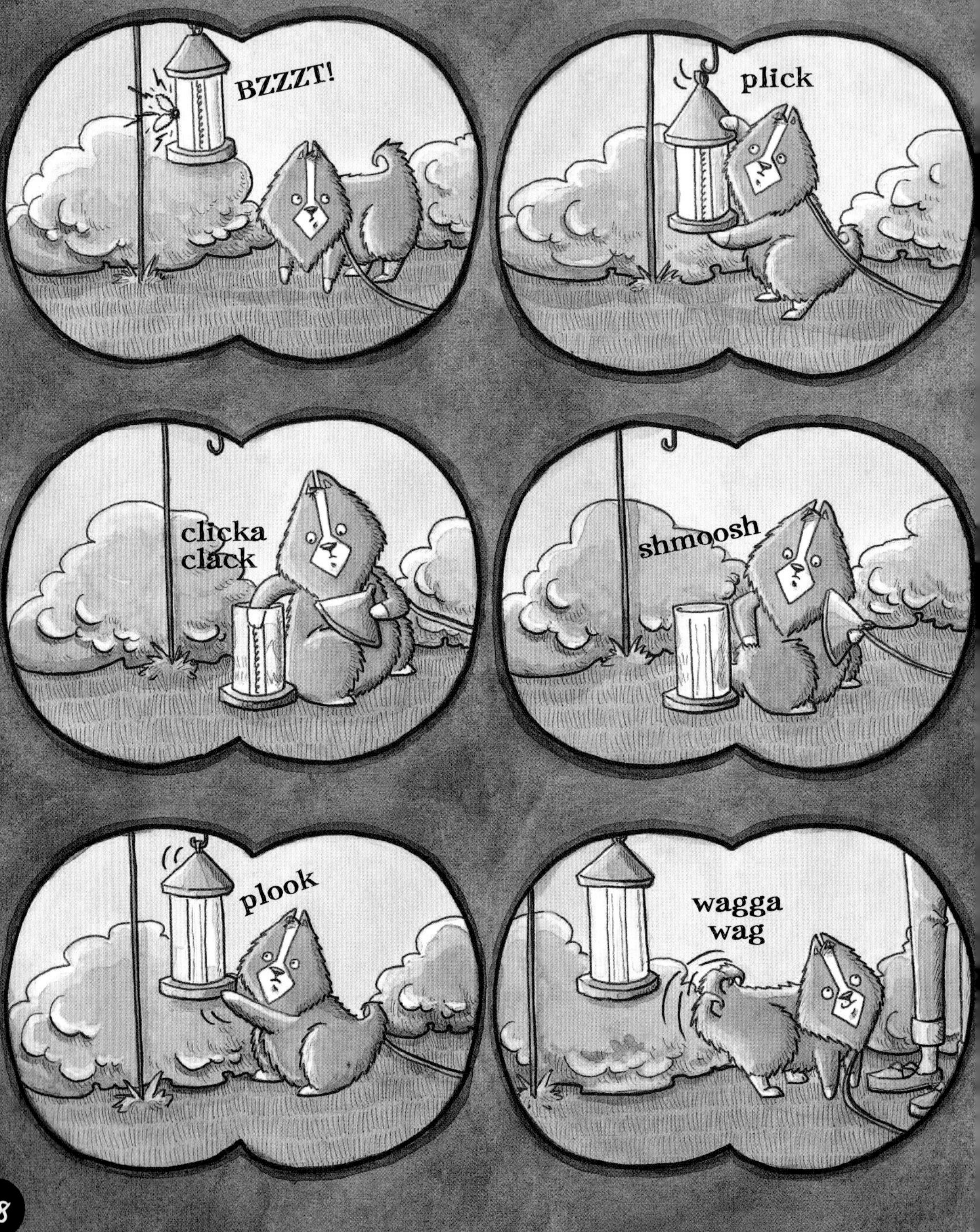
BZZZT!
plick
clicka clack
shmoosh
plook
wagga wag

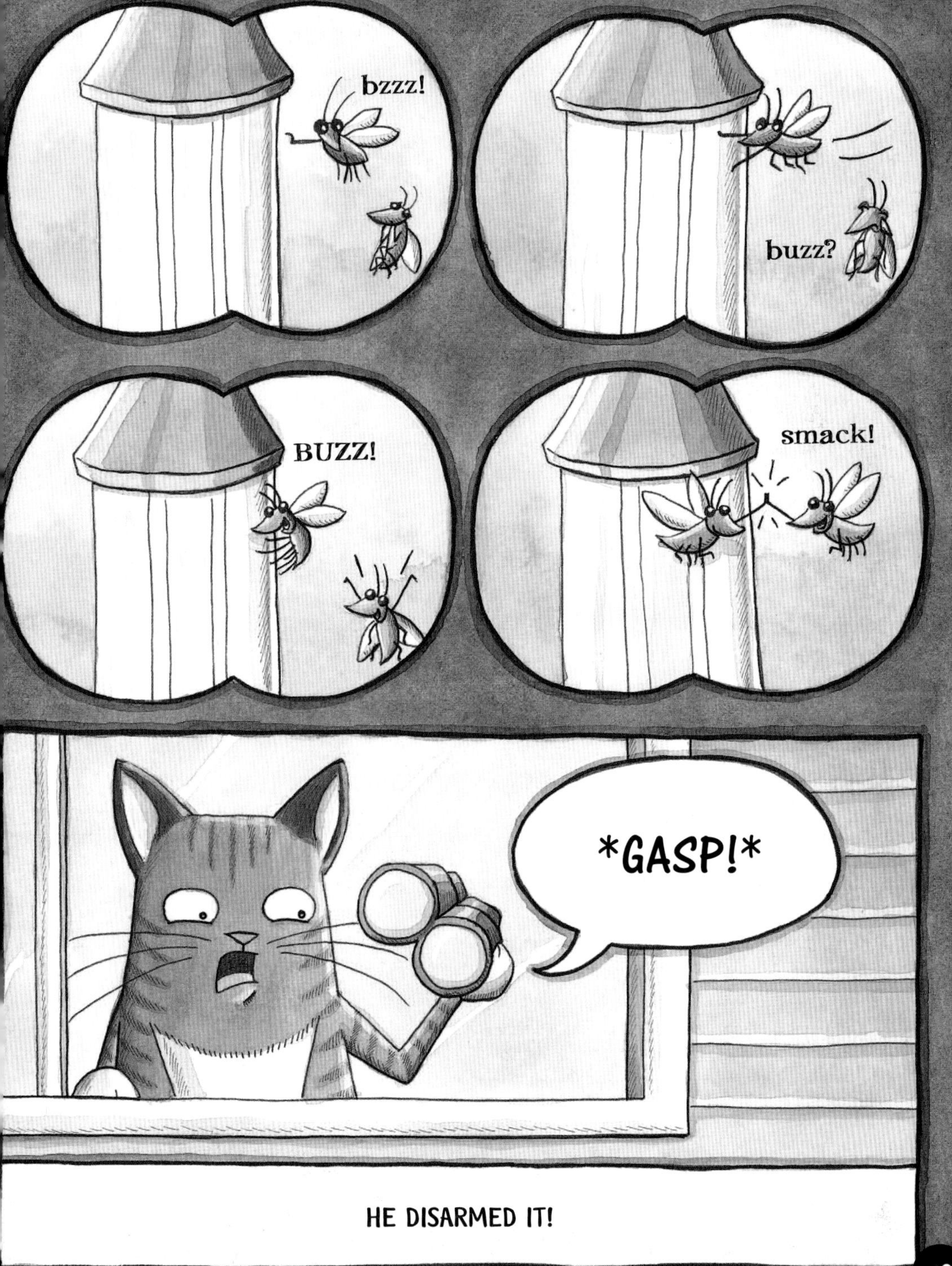

bzzz!
buzz?
BUZZ!
smack!
GASP!
HE DISARMED IT!

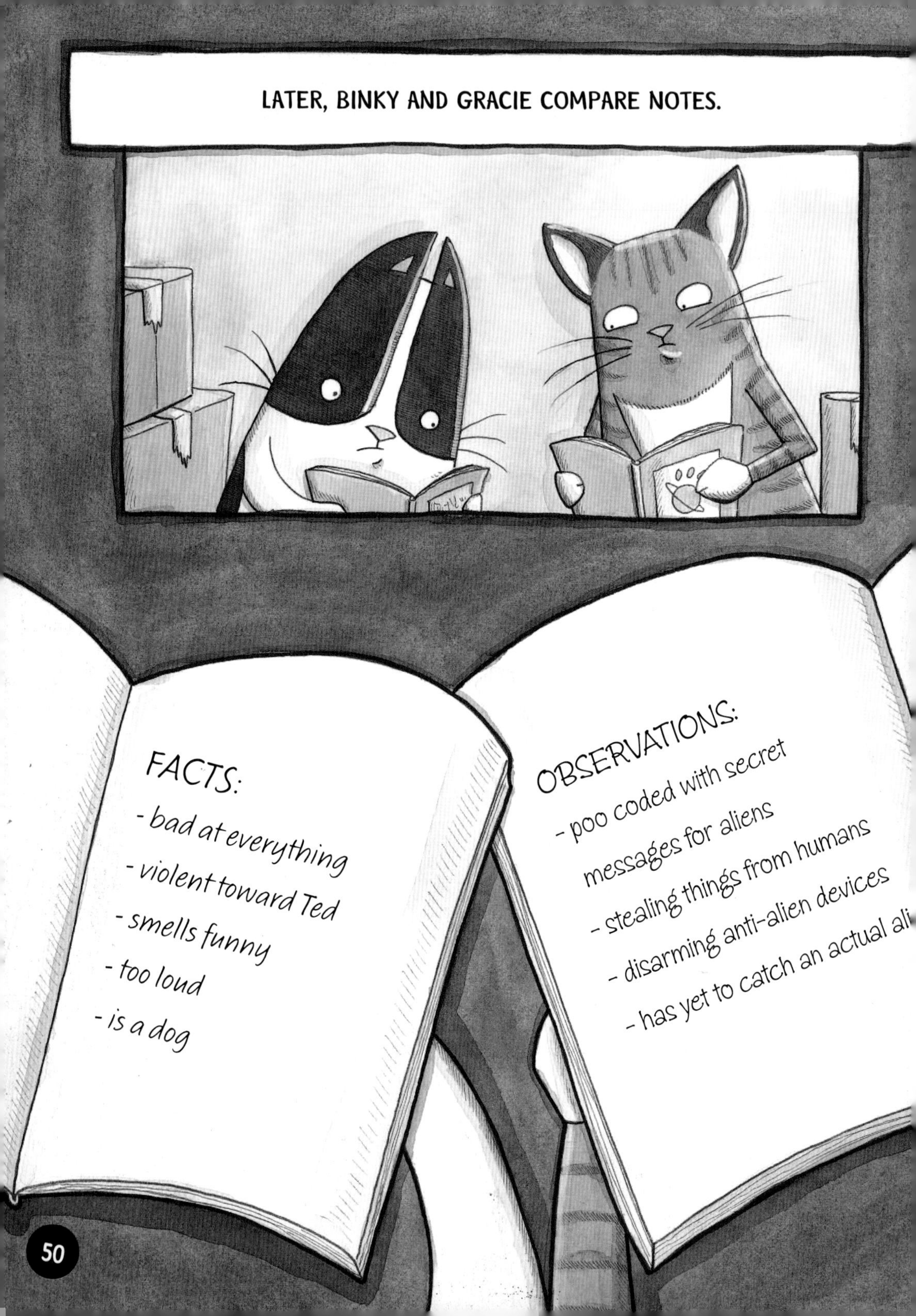
LATER, BINKY AND GRACIE COMPARE NOTES.
FACTS:
- bad at everything
- violent toward Ted
- smells funny
- too loud
- is a dog
OBSERVATIONS:
- poo coded with secret messages for aliens
- stealing things from humans
- disarming anti-alien devices
- has yet to catch an actual ali

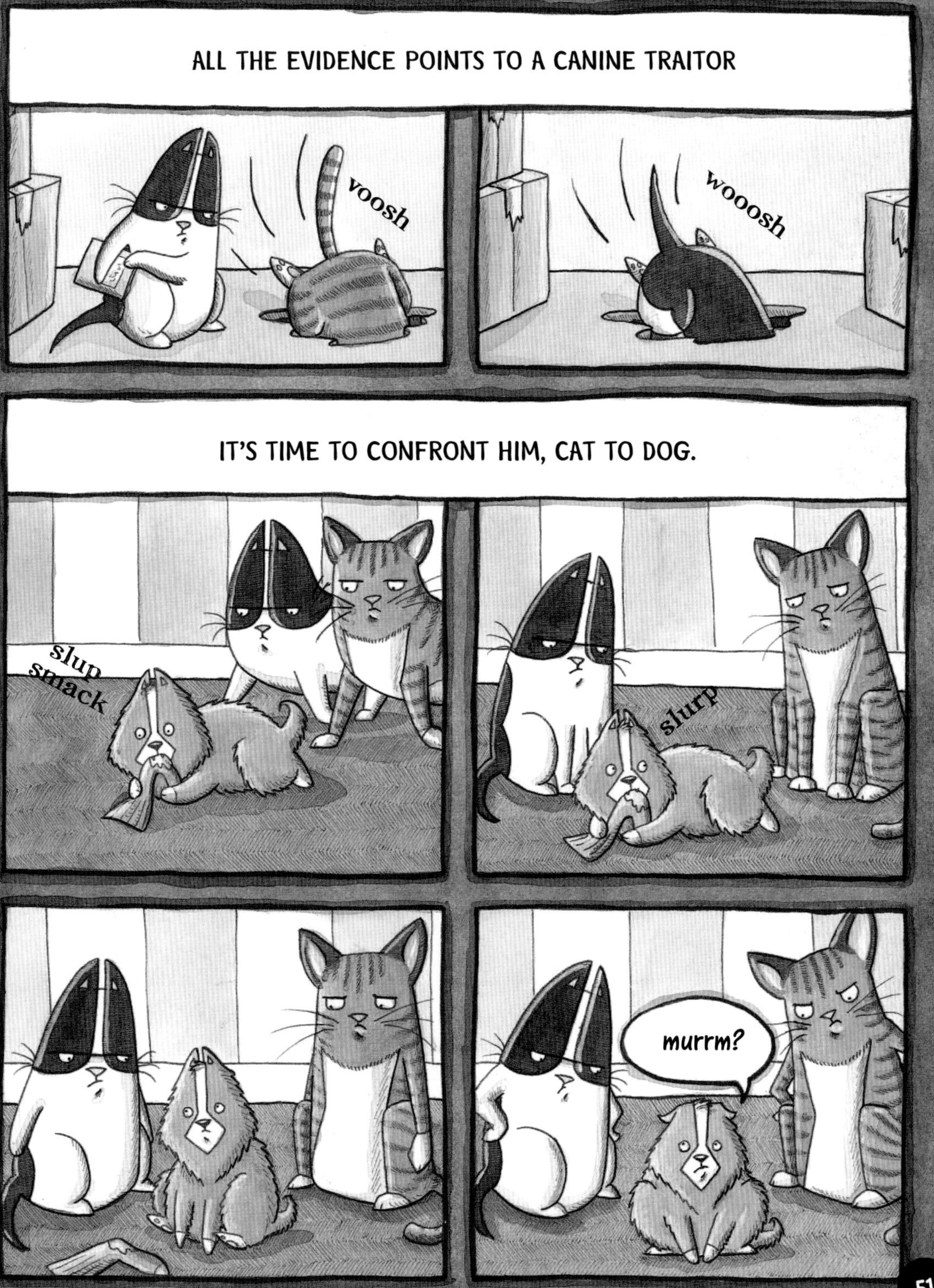
ALL THE EVIDENCE POINTS TO A CANINE TRAITOR
voosh
wooosh
IT'S TIME TO CONFRONT HIM, CAT TO DOG.
slup
smack
slurp
murrm?

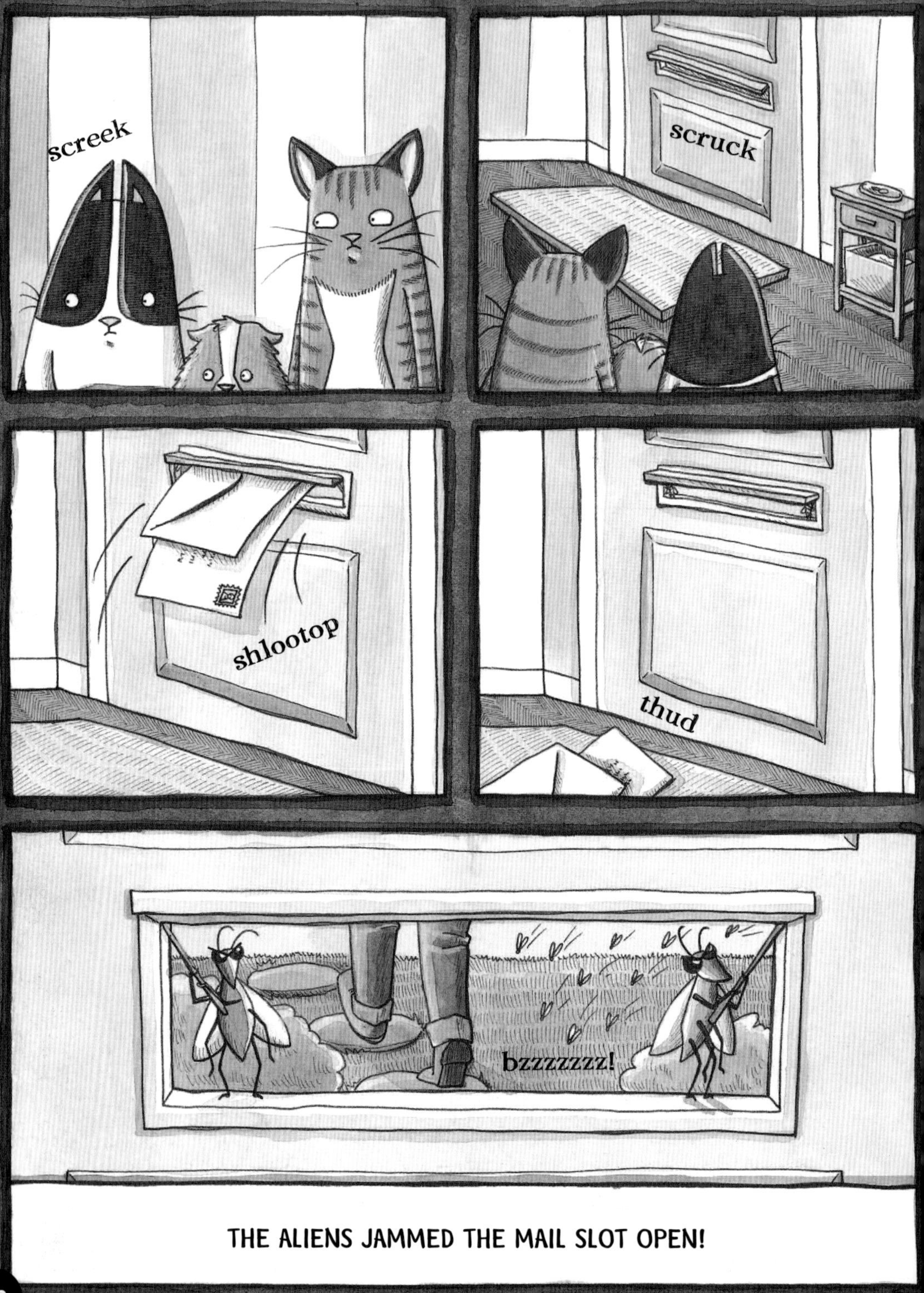
screek
scruck
shlootop
thud
bzzzzzz!
THE ALIENS JAMMED THE MAIL SLOT OPEN!

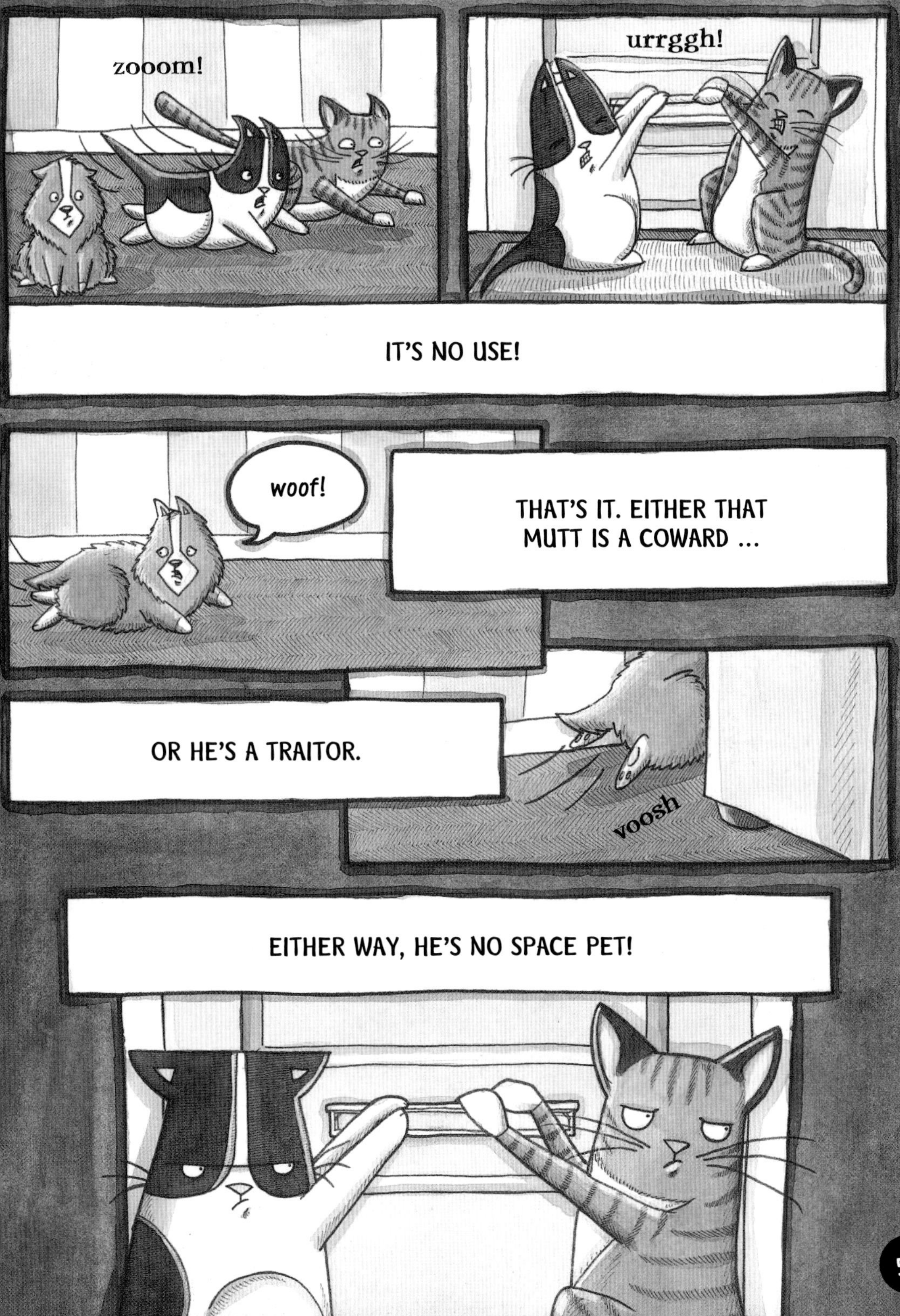
zooom!
urrggh!
IT'S NO USE!
woof!
THAT'S IT. EITHER THAT MUTT IS A COWARD ...
OR HE'S A TRAITOR.
voosh
EITHER WAY, HE'S NO SPACE PET!

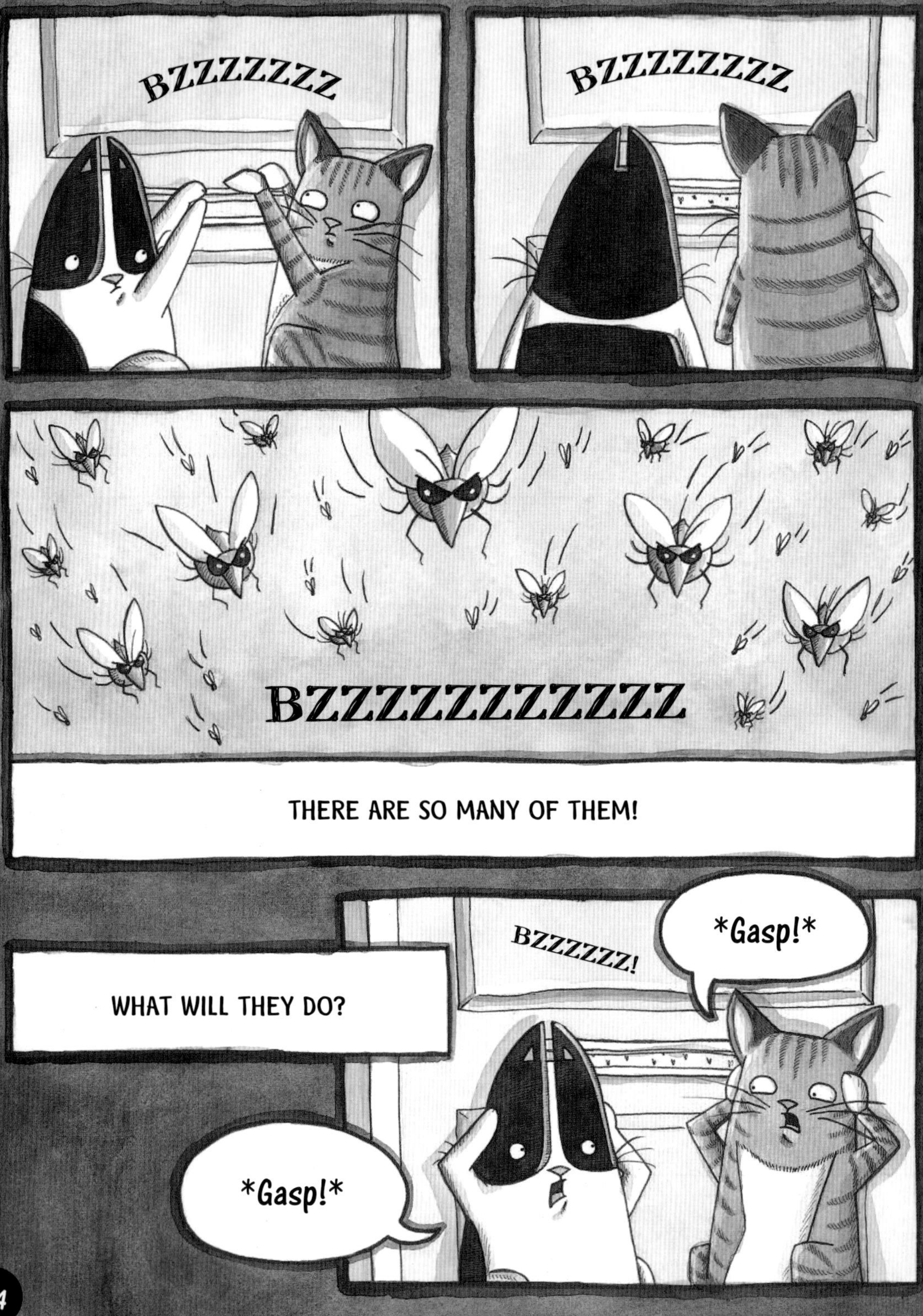
BZZZZZZZ
BZZZZZZZZ
BZZZZZZZZZZZZ
THERE ARE SO MANY OF THEM!
WHAT WILL THEY DO?
BZZZZZZ!
Gasp!
Gasp!

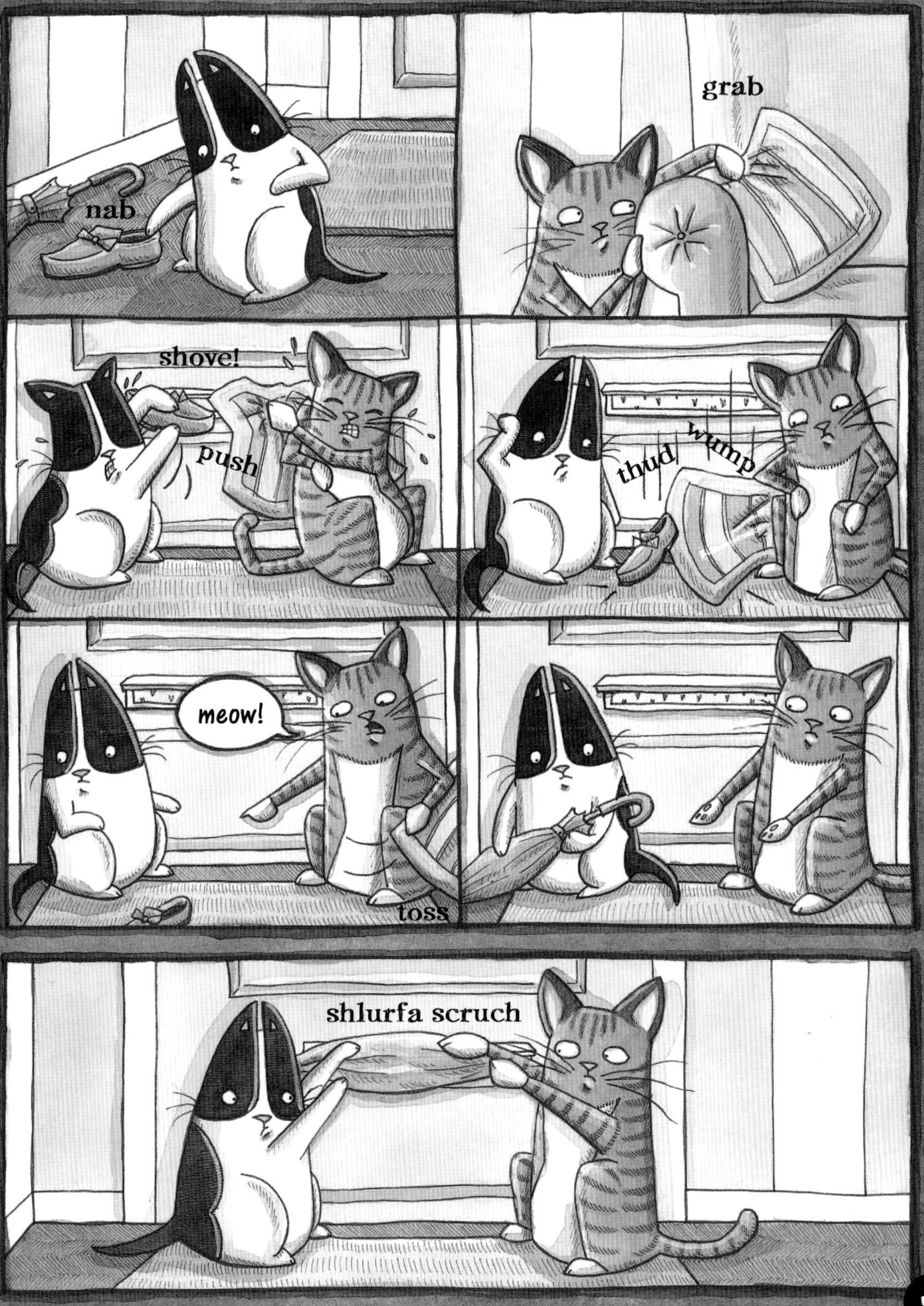
nab
grab
shove!
push
thud
wump
meow!
toss
shlurfa scruch

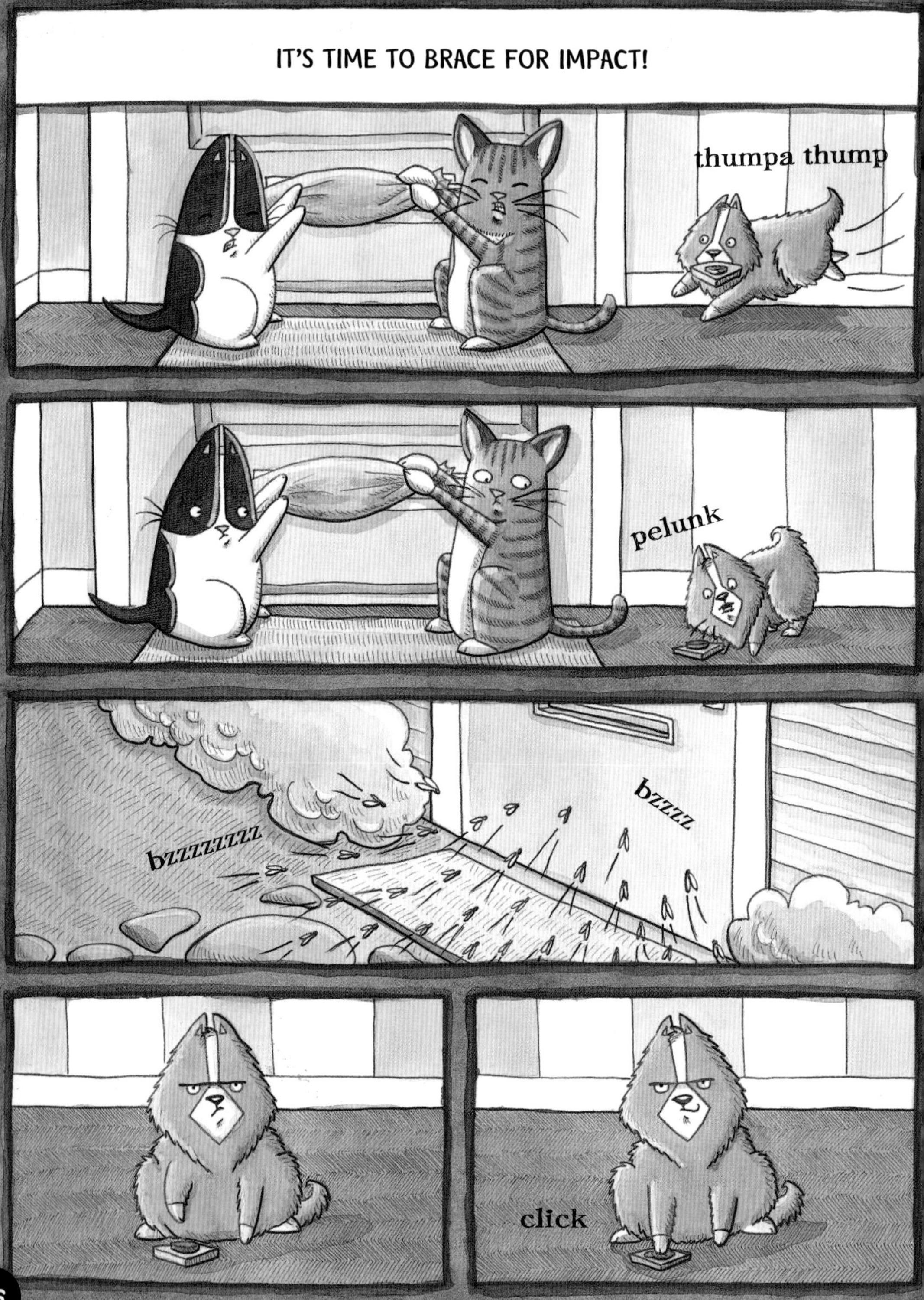
IT'S TIME TO BRACE FOR IMPACT!
thumpa thump
pelunk
bzzzzzzz
bzzzz
click

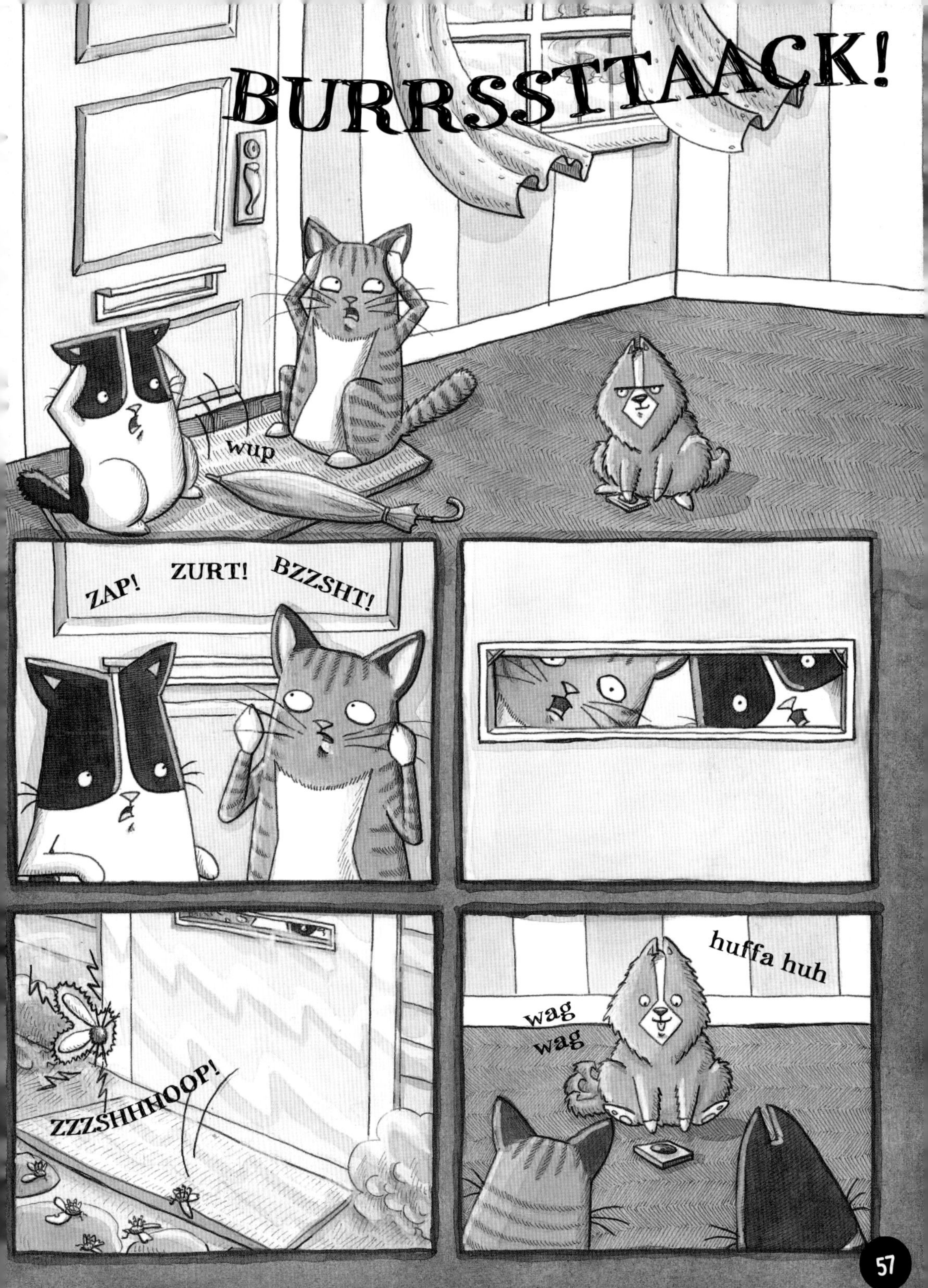
BURRSSTTAACK!
wup
ZAP!
ZURT!
BZZSHT!
ZZZSHHHOOP!
huffa huh
wag
wag

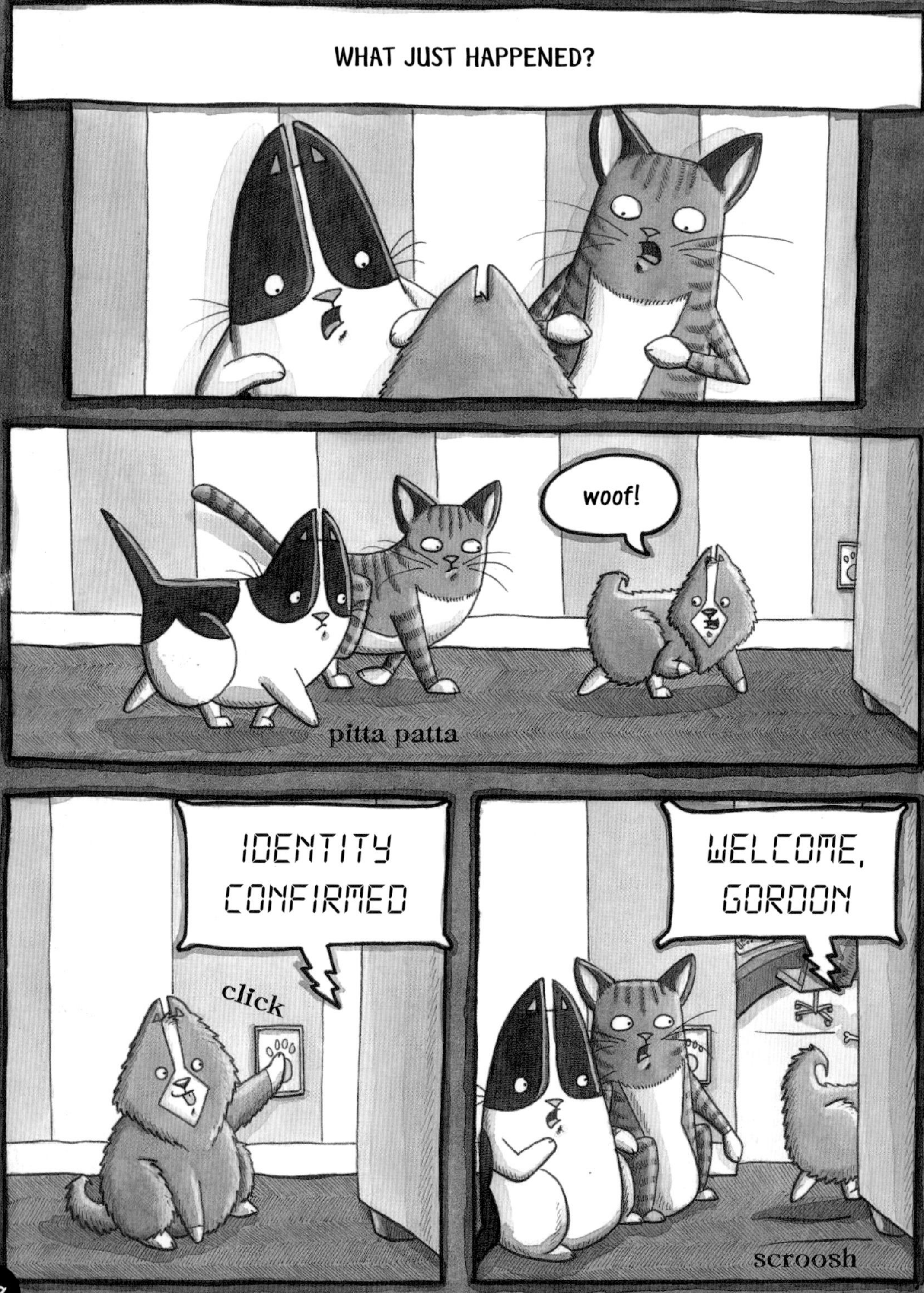

WHAT JUST HAPPENED?
woof!
pitta patta
IDENTITY CONFIRMED
click
WELCOME, GORDON
scroosh

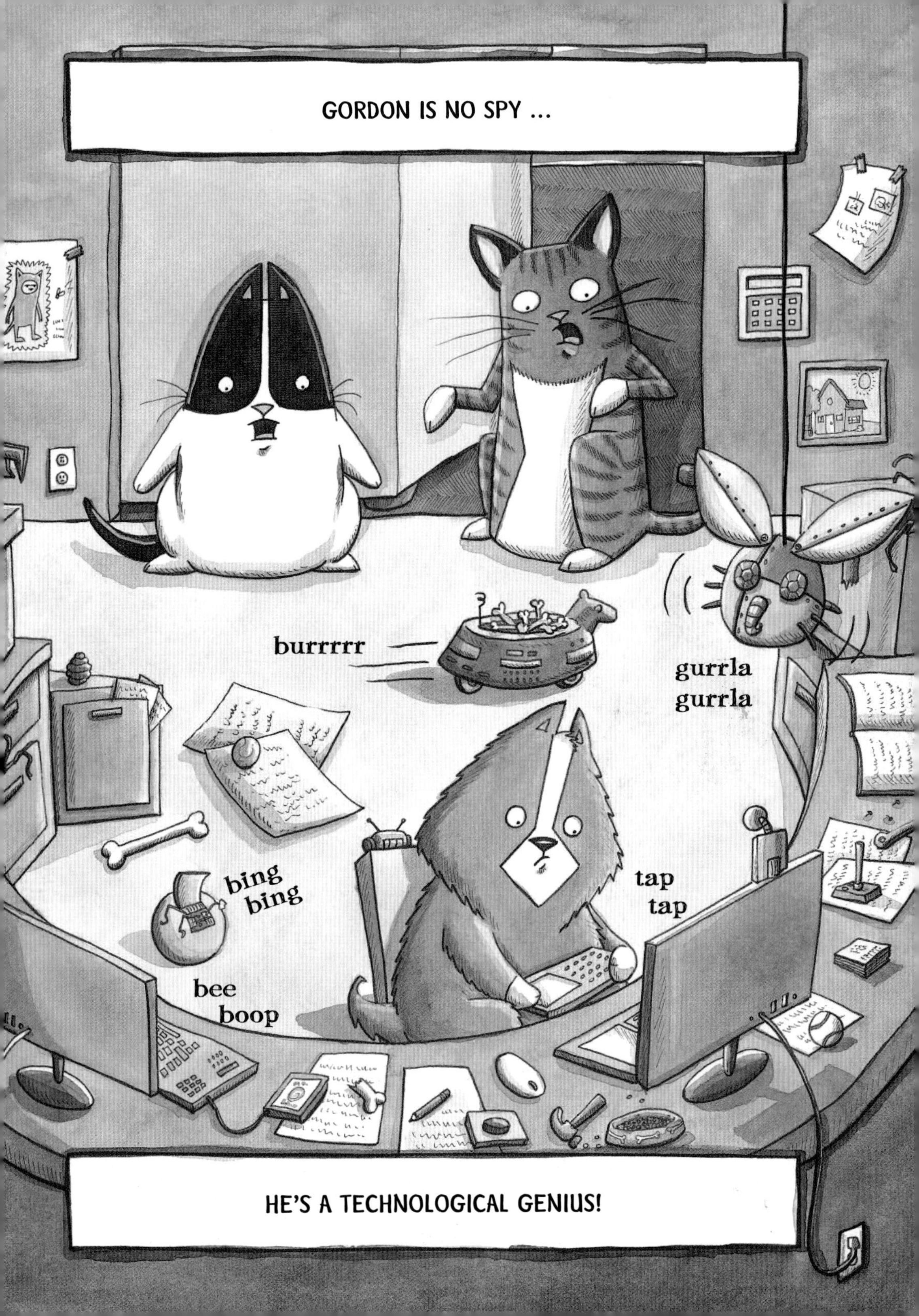
GORDON IS NO SPY ...
burrrrr
gurrla
gurrla
bing
bing
tap
tap
bee
boop
HE'S A TECHNOLOGICAL GENIUS!

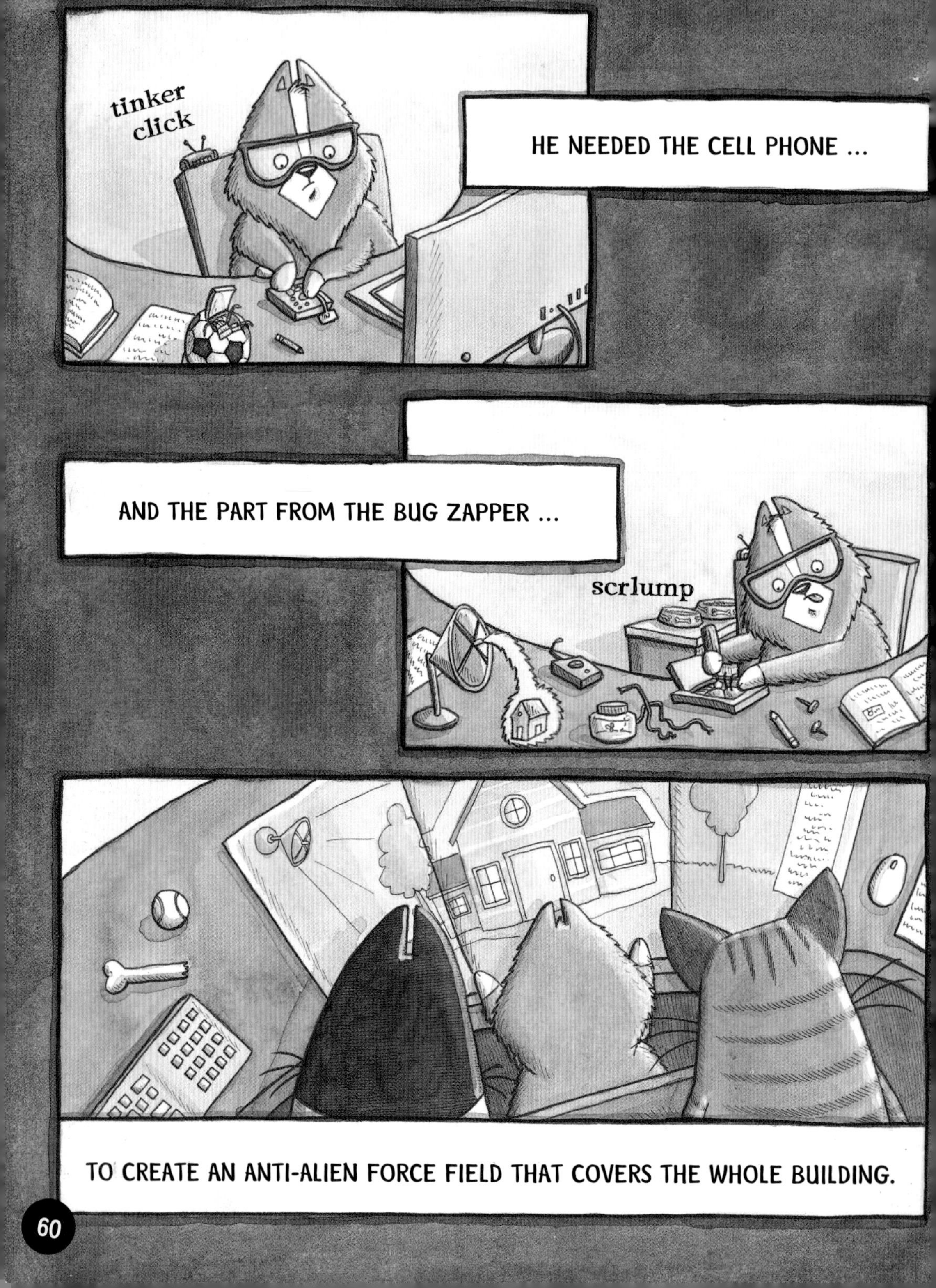
tinker
click
HE NEEDED THE CELL PHONE ...
AND THE PART FROM THE BUG ZAPPER ...
scrlump
TO CREATE AN ANTI-ALIEN FORCE FIELD THAT COVERS THE WHOLE BUILDING.

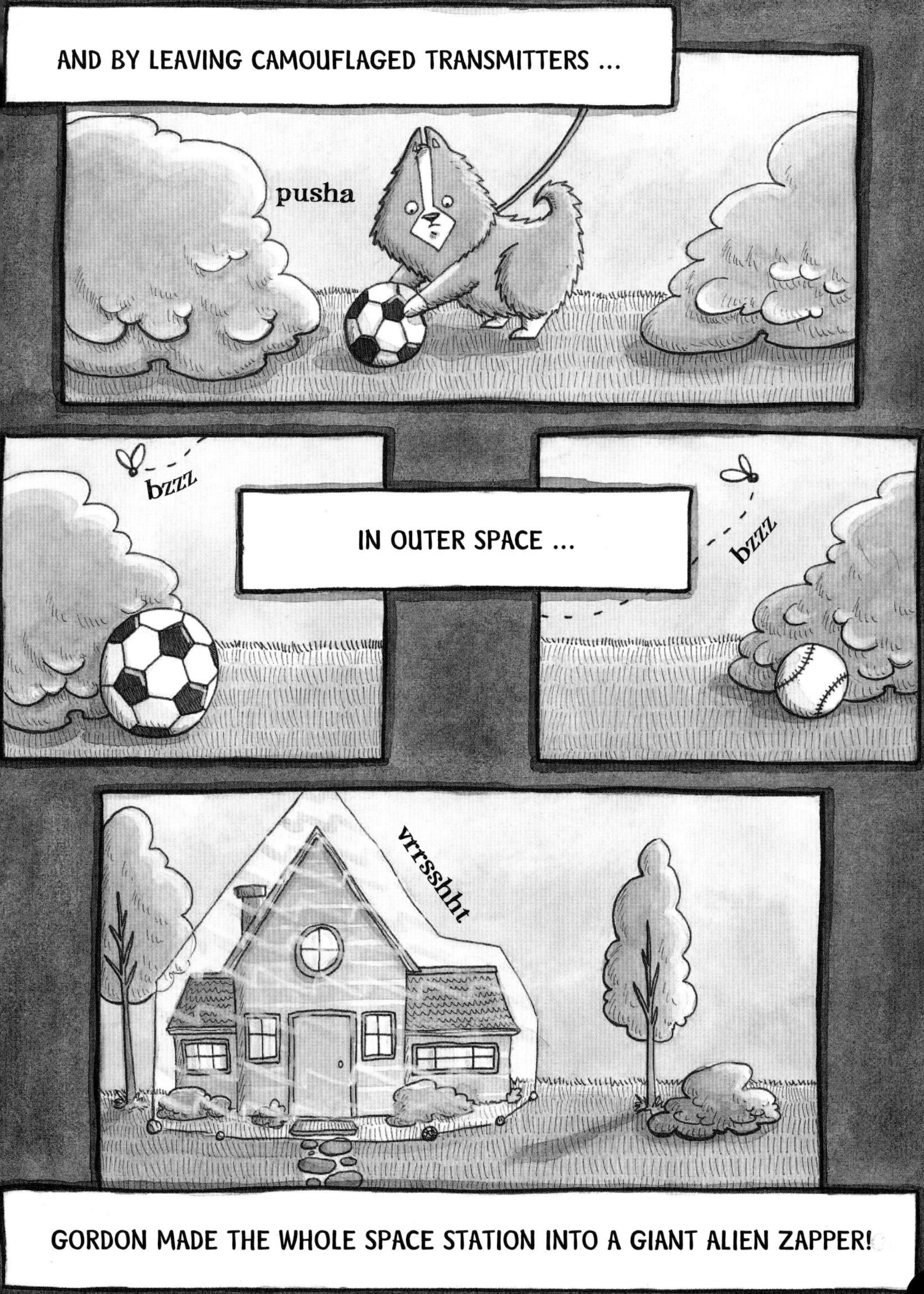
AND BY LEAVING CAMOUFLAGED TRANSMITTERS ...
pusha
bzzz
IN OUTER SPACE ...
bzzz
vrrsshht
GORDON MADE THE WHOLE SPACE STATION INTO A GIANT ALIEN ZAPPER!

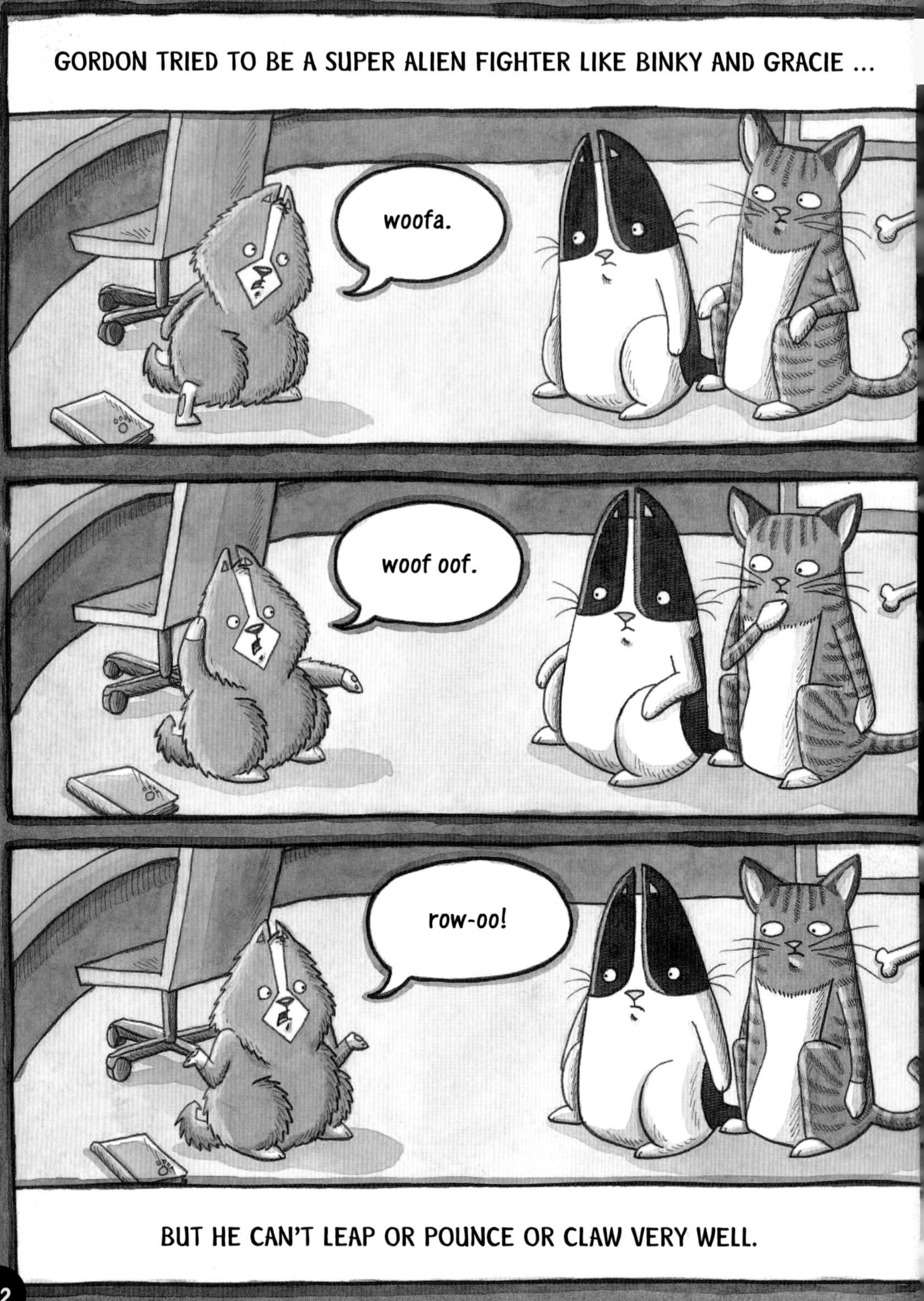
GORDON TRIED TO BE A SUPER ALIEN FIGHTER LIKE BINKY AND GRACIE ...
woofa.
woof oof.
row-oo!
BUT HE CAN'T LEAP OR POUNCE OR CLAW VERY WELL.

WHAT HE *CAN* DO ...

flup

IS USE HIS MIND TO MAKE THE SPACE STATION SAFER FOR ALL OF THEM.

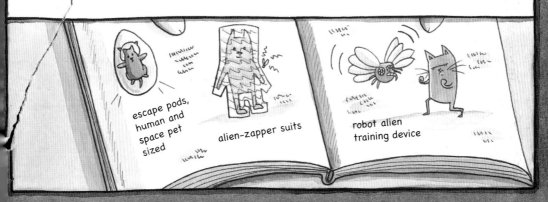

escape pods,
human and
space pet
sized

alien-zapper suits

robot alien
training device

slurp!

BINKY WAS WRONG ABOUT THIS CANINE CADET.

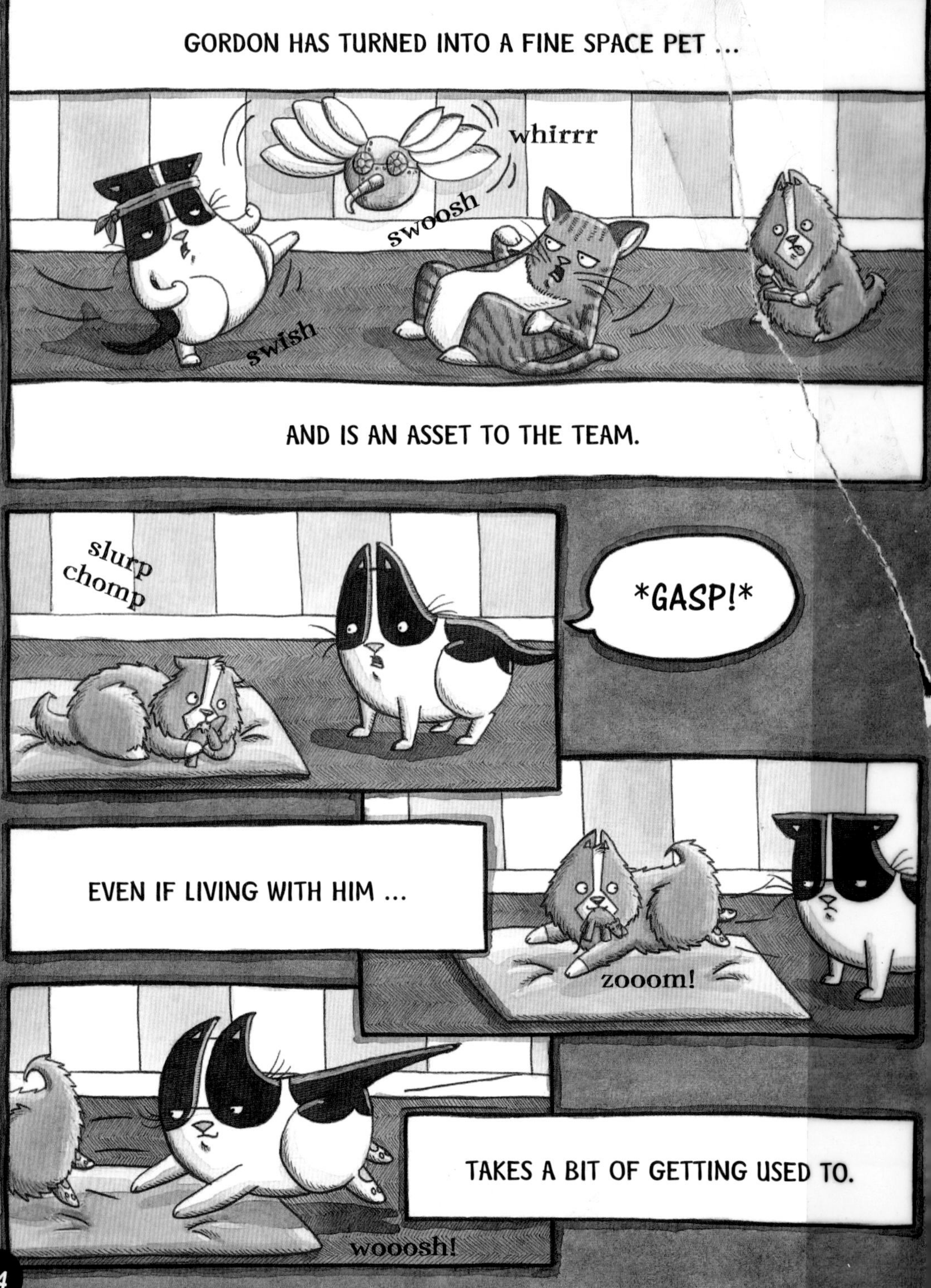
GORDON HAS TURNED INTO A FINE SPACE PET ...
whirrr
swoosh
swish
AND IS AN ASSET TO THE TEAM.
slurp
chomp
GASP!
EVEN IF LIVING WITH HIM ...
zooom!
TAKES A BIT OF GETTING USED TO.
wooosh!